D1738461

Also by Sue Perkins: Allen's Mother is Waiting

SCHWINN BLACK PHANTOM

What happened in 1949;
We kept to ourselves

SUE PERKINS

Order this book online at www.trafford.com
or email orders@trafford.com

Most Trafford titles are also available at major online book retailers.

Printed in the United States of America.

ISBN: 978-1-4669-2131-3 (sc)
ISBN: 978-1-4669-2133-7 (hc)
ISBN: 978-1-4669-2132-0 (e)

Library of Congress Control Number: 2012905395

Trafford rev. 03/21/2012

www.trafford.com

North America & international
toll-free: 1 888 232 4444 (USA & Canada)
phone: 250 383 6864 ♦ fax: 812 355 4082

The Author wishes to thank:

My daughter, Leslie, for her unfaltering willingness
to lend a hand with technical details
My husband, Lee, for a man's point of view
Leslie Christensen and Jeff King
for allowing Samson to be a hero in this tale

In memory of Lee,
whose gentle, male voice threads throughout these pages

THE LAND OF COUNTERPANE

When I was sick and lay a-bed
I had two pillows at my head,
And all my toys beside me lay
To keep me happy all the day.

And sometimes for an hour or so
I watched my leaden soldiers go,
With different uniforms and drills,
Among the bed-clothes, through the hills;

And sometimes sent my ships in fleets
All up and down among the sheets;
Or brought my trees and houses out,
And planted cities all about.

I was the giant great and still
That sits upon the pillow-hill,
And sees before him, dale and plain,
The pleasant land of counterpane.

Robert Louis Stevenson

1

ARE YOU A MAN OR A MOUSE?

I'm too old for this, but Whitey Swift just phoned me a few minutes ago to remind me that the Woodard property is still up for sale, and that I'd best get my tired ass in gear if we're going to "gitter dun." I don't make hasty decisions, and I usually have to sleep on things before I make a move. That can mean weeks. The unappreciative second Woodard generation took over the place when their stubborn daddy, Simon Woodard, died in his bed in his nineties. Whitey, who keeps me informed about the neighborhood, says that Simon had refused to go to any stinky old people's warehouse. "I ain't ever peed my pants, and I can still fix myself a sandwich and do the Sunday crossword puzzle." I remember the spectacle of Simon driving into town backwards on his John Deere when his car wouldn't start. The only gear he could get the tractor into was reverse, so he backed that sucker down Bloom Street, hung a right on Maine and took a wide, backward left down Dragster's Boulevard and backed it diagonally in front of Lester Drew's Tavern next to the Sheriff's office.

I had moved out of that neighborhood into a bungalow near the Aksarben racetrack (Aksarben, being Nebraska spelled backward) when I got married, but Whitey stayed in Florence and still resides on Annie Belle Drive with his wife. We're both the same age, 62, and our offspring are all grown and fixing their own meals and raising their own kids. Whitey sometimes calls me THUMP, and you will find out later why. My real name is Warren Hearst.

The Woodard property is out on the northern skirts of Florence, a small community on the north end of Omaha. The white farmhouse with the big front porch sits on Spirit Hill Drive that angles southwest off Bloom Street. When you sit on Woodard's porch swing, you look right across the road at Spirit Hill Cemetery. In his younger days, when Whitey and I were ten and going into the fifth grade at Bloom Elementary, Simon was tending a full apple orchard, raising pumpkins, corn and tomatoes, which he would sell in season. I have a hunch that his wife, Eunice, did a lot of canning.

Anyway, as I was saying, (I tend to go down other roads sometimes, and you'll have to forgive me) after the old man died, his kids moved out there with good intentions of fixing the place up. I should tell you, it really needs attention, according to Whitey. He says that they probably decided that the cost of the renovation wasn't worth it, and that the next Junior League Woodard generation coming up wouldn't touch it with a ten foot pole. Now, it's sitting out there in the boonies, watching the town build closer and eventually swallow it. It's all bound up with weeds and vines, and the barn doors are drooping and ready to fall off. If I was buried in that cemetery across the road, I'd be upset as hell at the view. I'm sure there's a developer waiting to pounce on the property and turn it into something akin to the houses on a monopoly game.

"The house is empty, and I think we should move on it before it gets too dicey. We don't move as fast as we did when we were ten. How 'bout we meet down at Bucky's place tomorrow morning about nine for a cuppa joe and lay out the plan?"

Whitey (His real name is Duane Swift, but I'll explain that later.) was always the one with the plan. Has been from that first life-altering day I met him. To this day, he's like a fart on a griddle when he decides to move forward on a thing. "The rumor in Florence is that the Woodard kids have gone south and left the place in the hands of the real estate company, and they didn't take a single thing with 'em off the property. I hear they're gonna have an estate sale."

"Sounds like it's now or not at all, doesn't it?" I'm wondering if I have the energy. As I'm talking to my old pal on the phone in the kitchen, I'm peering out the window in the early evening dusk of the back yard. All the time Whitey is convincing me to move on it, I'm thinking about the consequences here with my neighbors. I could be in hot water with the Swans, Rose and Wilber, who live next door south of me. He spends hours sitting on the ground, pulling weeds or any other foreign thing out of his manicured blue grass, and Rose tends her flowers and shines her windows with Windex all day. Nice people, though, and I'll cross that bridge when I get to it, I suppose. I have to admit that I'm on edge about this harebrained scheme, even though it was my own idea. I made the mistake of bouncing it off Whitey, and he just ran with it.

"Lemme check my date book." Whitey waits patiently on the other end of the phone, knowing damn well that all of the little squares on my BOULTON HARDWARE calendar are blank in the month of March.

"Can you **sandwich** me in at nine tomorrow mornin'?"

"You bet." The phone clicks and is silent. Whitey hangs up when he thinks there aren't any more possible words to say about a thing.

◆   ◆   ◆

I live in *old* Omaha, where the trees could be older than I am, and you can find a corner grocery store a couple of blocks away. It's quiet here with very few small children. There aren't any covenants about fences or sheds and the like. The University campus isn't far, and the students look to be about twelve.

Ten years ago this spring, Gwen, the love of my life and the mother of my beautiful daughter, Wendy, was crossing the street down by the grocery store, when one of those students ran a red light and snuffed out her life. Just like that. She had gone to pick up some of the makings for vegetable soup, my favorite. My beautiful wife hung on for a couple of days, while Wendy and I held her hands on each side of the hospital bed, praying, crying and talking to her. Hoping. Then the Good Lord took her. I guess it must have been for the best, but it was the worst thing I ever went through in my life. I thank God for my daughter and Bernie, my sweet grandson. They make me want to live. I haven't been able to move away from this house, and why should I? I love this old neighborhood.

Whitey likes the small town atmosphere where we grew up, so he has stayed in Florence. We have been close friends all these years, even though we live several miles apart on opposite ends of Omaha. He married Connie, a spitfire, take-charge sort of gal. Connie was a classmate of ours. Whitey and Connie have five kids, born in about the same amount of years. They all grew up in a bunch, and all left the house almost at the same time. *Gitter dun.* Connie informed Whitey that the fifth one was the caboose, and she got something done to make sure of it.

It's my guess that she figured Whitey's machinery would never break down. Whitey and Connie are eighteen-time grandparents.

My beautiful Wendy made me a grandpa once. A son, named Bernard, after my father. Bernie is one of the great joys of my life and is now twelve. Gwen and I had gone to K.C. in order to be there at his birth. I can still hear those little, high-pitched cries when he was born. If all the babies in that hospital nursery cried at once, I would have been able to pick out my grandson's cry. Wendy is divorced from the son-of-a-bitch who ran out on her when Bernie was six months old. She lives not far from me and has never married.

My kitchen smells like meat loaf microwave dinner, and I'm heading out the side door for a breath of fresh air. I'm pushing the screened door open, when Barnabus streaks through on to the linoleum and straight to the top of the refrigerator, via the counter by the sink, where he waits for the can opener to access the tuna. Albacore in water. Won't eat the cheap stuff. He's a gray tabby, weighing in at eighteen pounds. Barnabus knows when it's Friday. It's the day he gets this special "people food."

I'm just taking my fiber therapy and tossing my relaxed-fit jeans over the bedroom chair, when Barnabus springs onto the bed, sabotaging the ritual of turning down the covers by attacking my hand and nosing under everything. There's now a lump under the blanket at the bottom of the bed, waiting for my vulnerable, bare foot. I know that in a few seconds he will be curled up in my armpit. Nothing like tuna breath in the night.

◆   ◆   ◆

It's Saturday, and the cat has been left *in* today with his rations. I left a load of my underwear in the machine, and I'm pulling into the parking lot on the windy, north side of Bucky's place. Whitey's red pickup truck is already there, and he's in our regular booth in the front window with a view of the sidewalk. Bucky's has been in business since I was a kid, and Petty has been waiting on us for at least fifteen years. She plunks my coffee down before my butt even hits the bench across from Whitey.

"Howze your buns, Cutie? The usual?"

"Eggs over medium, white toast, two strips, real crisp." Petty bends over so that her bright red lips are close to my hearing aid. Her generous busts are right *there.*

"I knew that." She whispers in her sexiest voice. I don't know her age. She's one of those timeless people. Probably had a lot of action back in the day. Possibly, even now. Petty Cash is her name, and I'm not sure I want to know how she got it. Whitey has waited quietly during this exchange. "She's probably been somewhere and back. You sure you don't wanna try your luck?"

Whitey is clicking his fingernails on the Formica table. It's a bad habit he has, and it drives me nuts. Sounds like a snare drum. It's a subconscious signal he's sending in order to get the conversation going about the *plan*. His technique is working, because I start talking just to shut up the noise.

"So, what are you having for breakfast?"

"Pancakes. Don't see 'em up there in the window yet. We gonna get it done this week?" *clickety clickety clickety*

I secretly have doubts about this whole caper. It came up a few months ago, when Whitey heard the skinny that the Woodards might be heading south forever.

"You sure they're gone for good? They're not coming back to take inventory of the house and the grounds?" I could picture the headlines: TWO OLD FARTS ARRESTED FOR TRESPASS, THEFT, DISTURBING THE PEACE

Whitey is leaning forward on his elbows, so that he sort of *plugs in* to my face and rivets me there. You just know you're going to be quiet and listen when he does that *thing.* He's been that way as long as I've known him. Whitey looks around to make sure that nobody can hear. "It's gotta be at night. REALLY night, like two or three AM. Ain't no other way. We take my truck, do the demo, load up, cover the stuff with a tarp, haul ass out of there and go like hell to your place. We unload in your garage, and I truck on home. Operation breakdown and transport complete."

Sounds too simple to me. I'm thinking about my bothersome hip and sore knees and Whitey's bad eyesight. The more I think about this, the dumber it sounds. Whitey's eyes are still looking right into my brain, while I'm processing this scenario. Petty is arriving with the vittles. She has two plates, balanced on one arm and the coffeepot in her other hand.

"There ya go guys. Need anything else?" We tell her no, and she's off in her side-to-side shuffle, as if she's been used to having men enjoy watching her walk away.

As if Whitey could hear my thoughts and doubts, he continues after Petty is out of hearing range. "You're gonna go chicken on me, right?"

I can't chicken out. This has been priority one in my mind since Wendy's jerk of a husband left her and the baby high and dry down in Kansas City. Glen, the A-Hole Orthodontist, had announced at the dinner table just before Christmas, that he needed some space and some time to find out who he was. I'll tell you who he was ... **a self-absorbed, cheating, womanizing snake-in-the-grass fast-laner, who raced around in his Porsche and blew off the fact that he was a father and husband.** He told Wendy that he didn't think he was cut out for fatherhood. He was right. I met my devastated daughter and my grandson at the airport within that week. We found a temporary apartment for them before the month was out, and they've been in Omaha since then. Wendy now has a nice home near the university, and, thanks to the divorce settlement and child support, they are financially okay. But, I can tell you one thing ... That maggot of an EX of hers had better not meet me in an alley.

"Count me in."

"We're doin' the right thing." Those disturbing eyes of Whitey's can really pin a guy down. So can his size and his strength, even though he is nearly sixty three. He was a state champion wrestler when we were seniors in high school. I, at one hundred seventy pounds, would not fare too well in a physical battle with Whitey, a solid two hundred weigh in. The pounds came on when he quit wrestling.

After three cups of Bucky's stout coffee, we've solved some of the world's problems and made a list on the paper placemats of the stuff needed for the upcoming caper. Between the two of us, we have flashlights, work gloves, claw hammers, saws, dark clothes, an extension ladder, some heavy rope, a large tarp and a six pack for the truck when we're done. *If we live through it and don't go to jail by being caught by the County Sheriff.*

"You sure it's still there?" I'm a number ten worrier.

We decide on the small hours of Tuesday morning. I mention to Whitey that we should probably break out the thermals, and he gives me that look I get, when he thinks I'm overworking the plan. That's the way I tend to be about everything, but Whitey flies by the seat of his pants.

Having tipped Petty and paid at the counter, we forge out the north door into the March wind and trudge toward our respective vehicles, my tan Buick LeSabre and Whitey's red Ford pickup.

"Don't forget a stocking cap. You'll glow like a beacon!"

"Yeah, yeah. At least I still *have* hair, buddy boy!"

I crawl into the Buick, and my clothes have that faint aroma of bacon. It's a satisfying feeling you get from Saturday morning breakfast. I don't miss the absence of the smoke that used to be part of the cafe atmosphere. I quit the killer habit when I married Gwen. Whitey never did smoke. He was a top athlete and wanted to be able to breathe and keep up with his grandchildren when he got older. Neither of us is upset with the new smoking laws.

Whitey is an albino with a thick mop of chalk white, unruly hair, a pink complexion and white eye lashes that don't do a very good job of shading those disturbing pink eyes. I take pride in my own curly, reddish gray, wiry fringe that looks like a nest for my shiny, bald head. Whitey has commented that I'm probably the senior Napoleon Dynamite.

2

WHEN YOU GOTTA GO, YOU GOTTA GO

I think it is plain old fate that put Whitey Swift into my pathetic life as a ten-year-old. Well, fate and my Mother. Dad didn't have to spend most of the day with me like Mom did, but he would kick in and do his bit after work and on week ends. I guess I should explain why I thought my life was so blamed miserable.

I had the shivers, nausea and a temperature. I was all bundled up in a blanket on the back seat of that '47 Fleetmaster Chevy Woody station wagon. My older sister, Beverly, was up front next to Dad. Mom was in the middle seat, so she could be closer to me and keep Beverly as far away from me as possible. Dad pushed it to the max all the way into Omaha, Nebraska at 50 miles per hour, which was about top speed for that wagon. We were coming in from Lexington, Nebraska, east on highway thirty. Mom kept looking back at me with her eyes about ready to spill over. She had filled a milk bottle with water and a straw, and every few minutes Mom's arm would arch over the seat back to where I was. I just gulped some of it down whenever I saw it coming. I was hot, cold, and hurting real bad, as Dad drove us through all those little farm towns along highway thirty. Kearney, Gibbon, Wood River, Grand Island, Columbus, Fremont, and each one of them had a grain elevator right next to the Union Pacific main line running parallel to the highway. "See those trees over there? That's the Platte River." Dad had a way of pointing out spots of interest, but I was too weak to sit up and look.

I had been diagnosed with Polio, and we were heading for Children's Hospital where there were more doctors with more experience. My sis kept reading those silly signs about a shaving product along the road. I didn't think they were as

8

funny as Beverly did. "Dad, get a load of that!" She would say every time she spotted one coming. You had to read all of the many signs to get the whole message, because they were "written in segments." Mom explained.

DOESN'T
KISS YOU
LIKE SHE
USETER?
PERHAPS SHE'S SEEN
A SMOOTHER ROOSTER!
BURMA SHAVE

Turns out, I spent several weeks in that Omaha hospital in quarantine and several more weeks at home in Lexington in quarantine with a big black **X** on our front door. Nobody wanted my snot or spit or pee touching anybody else, and Beverly kept a good distance from me. Mom and Dad came close because they had to and wanted to. Beverly came down with what they thought was a little case of the flu, but the Doc said it could have been a mild case of the same stuff I had, only not so bad. Long story short, I came out with a damn gimpy leg with a brace on it. I could have wound up in an iron lung or a wheel chair or even worse … dead.

But I didn't. The doctor told me I was one of the lucky ones. I remember watching movies on a special projector that put the show on the ceiling, which allowed me to watch from my bed.

Beverly and I weren't in on the folk's decision to move to Omaha permanently. My unhappy sis, at age sixteen, would be leaving all of her high school friends. I heard a lot of sobbing and stomping around before we left. "Why can't I just stay in Lexington and live with Aunt Mary, so I can finish school with my *friends?*" As I look back on those days, I know it had to be hard as hell for Beverly to say goodbye to her friends at that age. As for me, I had made up my mind never to go back to school again, no matter where we lived. I didn't want to face any of my pals, especially the ones on the baseball team, sneaking peeks at me and feeling sorry for me, as I clumped around with my leg brace and my crutch. I didn't want to look at anybody and didn't want anybody looking at me, especially in a new, frightening school full of strangers. I hated life and my crummy body that wouldn't do what I wanted it to do. I was a miserable *crip*. I would go live in a shack in the mountains and kill my own food forever. I would be a hermit.

That final journey to Omaha was in the spring of '49. I was a scared ten-year-old, heading into fifth grade in a new, big town. I had missed a couple of months of the fourth grade, but I remember my teacher, Miss Ryan, saying, "There's no reason to hold Warren back, Mr. and Mrs. Hearst. School has always been easy for him, and he gets A's all the time, as you well know from his report cards!" She always bragged about me to my folks, but she didn't know my plans to run away into the wilderness, never to be heard from again. She would have been disappointed to hear that.

My dad had a way of forgetting about bodily functions when we traveled, and was not ever happy when one of us had to pee, especially if it was one of the women. I wish I had a dollar every time my dad would pull off the road and point out an old, empty school house or a barn and say, "Don't take too long, ladies." I still have that vision of Mom and Beverly high-stepping it through the weeds, carrying their roll of toilet paper and disappearing behind the old Public School number, whatever it was, in the middle of nowhere. "I wish there were nice, clean bathrooms along these roads, Bernie. Maybe someday after we're all dead and gone ..." My mother would say this often on road trips. She then would go on and on, speculating about the *FUTURE*.

Gone for only a few minutes, Mom and Sis would return to the car. There were explosive sighs as their behinds hit the leather car seats, once again, and off we would go. Left behind, would usually be two puddles ... one in the dust by my back door and one on the ground on the driver's side, deposited by Dad. This trip was a little different, since I had to pee in a coffee can, which was several times because of all that water. Intake—Output

> **ON CURVES AHEAD**
> **REMEMBER, SONNY**
> **THAT RABBIT'S FOOT**
> **DIDN'T SAVE**
> **THE BUNNY BURMA-SHAVE**

Back in Lexington, Dad had turned his auto parts business and service station over to my uncle and found a job with another similar company in Omaha. Those were the days when the attendant ran out the door in trousers with a crease up the leg, his clean shirt with his name on it and his service station cap with a bill. The attendant would say "Fill 'er up?", and you got your headlights shined, your tires checked, your windows cleaned and your tank full for a couple of bucks. He would even cash a check for you. As a kid, I loved that smell of gasoline and the stuff they used to clean the windshield and the squeaky sound it made when the man shined the glass … good memories of me on errands with my dad. I couldn't wait to get tall enough to roll my shirt sleeve up and rest my arm on the open window with my elbow sticking out like Dad's did. I remember the curly, red hairs on his beefy, left arm blowing in the wind.

In Omaha at last, we rented a furnished apartment for a couple of months. At first, it smelled like something between wet dog hair and egg salad, but Mom's bucket and mop and the SPIC 'N SPAN eventually made the place smell more like us. It wasn't long before there was a two-bedroom bungalow in our future. I remember how excited Mom was when she and Dad came home from house hunting on a Saturday. Beverly was in the apartment babysitting with me. I hated the word *babysitting*. I was ten! We ate bologna sandwiches and milk, listened to LET'S PRETEND on the radio and played Chinese checkers. I had my Tom Mix comic books, and Sis looked at the Sears Catalog. Beverly was nice to me most of the time, a good sis who hadn't made any new friends yet.

When Mom said that the house had two bedrooms, my sister and I started squabbling about the ownership of that second bedroom. Dad cut us off in the middle of it when he calmly announced, "There's an attic." Then the squabble really escalated, because now that second bedroom didn't sound near as interesting. The THIRD bedroom was the *attic*, and I wanted it real bad! So did Beverly. I pitched a real fit about it. I remember how that conversation went to this day.

"I don't want you to have to fight with that leg brace on those steep stairs, Warren."

"I can do it, Ma! I'm gonna have to walk up *stairs* in that stupid new school!"

It temporarily had slipped my mind that I would be living as a hermit in the mountains by the time school had started. Beverly, who had been pouting with her arms crossed in that perturbed position that I had seen so many times, argued something about being sixteen and getting to have first choice and needing a place for slumber parties.

"You always get what you want."

"No, I don't. YOU always get all the attention now, because you got *sick*!"

"Do not!"

"Do too."

That's how that all went, and I'll never forget my mother sidling over to Beverly, acting like she was going to tell her a secret. "You know, my dear, sweet daughter ... now that I think of it, that musty old attic is certainly not very handy to the *downstairs* telephone for a young lady with such big social plans."

Dad just stood there smiling at me. I loved my folks.

3

HUMDINGER HIDEAWAY

On moving day, I remember Dad waking me up about dawn. I had been sleeping on the living room sofa in the apartment, since Beverly got the second bedroom. You can't win 'em all, but I had won the *ATTIC* argument. I had put the idea of disappearing into the mountains off to the side temporarily. I reasoned that there was nothing wrong with enjoying the good things that came along in the middle of the crummy stuff. I could justify taking a vacation from being habitually cranky.

**FOR EARLY
MORNING
PEP AND BOUNCE
A BRAND NEW PRODUCT
WE ANNOUNCE
BURMA-SHAVE LOTION**

We took turns in the bathroom. Mom was in the kitchen, throwing odds and ends of food from the ice box into a grocery sack, and our "apartment clothes" went into the same kind of paper luggage. We stuffed all of our bags into the rear seat of the wagon, and Dad hauled us all to a dumpy little place called Bucky's in Florence for a real "out to eat" breakfast. Eating out rarely happened then. Beverly was talking non-stop about her new bedroom and how she was going to arrange it. She seemed to have forgotten her own grief about leaving her friends for the time being. I remember her saying that she couldn't wait to plug in her radio, turn the dial to the cool music station and arrange her new room. I had my own plans to find places for my own junk. I might also oil my mitt, even though I probably never would use it again, because I wouldn't be talking to anybody or seeing anybody or playing any baseball. I would have my comic books ... Hopalong Cassidy, Western Hero and Tom Mix with their guns blazing and their horses rearing up on the book covers. That's what I would do when I grew up. I

13

would be able to defy gravity and keep my balance, while I stood on top of a galloping horse, fighting the bad guys. I could even hang out the side of a fast-moving stage coach with one hand and shoot a gun with the other … never falling off. That was my dream, before the crummy polio got me.

With our stomachs full of pancakes, we pulled into the driveway at 2502 Bloom Street. It was a white bungalow with a front porch. Over the porch was a window under the front peak of the roof. It looked out over the roof of the porch, the front yard and the street. My very own lookout. The people had left the swing, and I recall Beverly squealing, "When I find a dream boat boy friend, we can sit out there in the summer and swing in the swing and smoooootch!" Dad didn't think that was funny.

"I think there are other things you should be thinking about, before that happens."

It took what seemed like forever for my Dad to unlock the front door. My parents had already seen the place, but not us kids. "One, two, three!" He said, and he swung it open in a big production way. Mom pointed Beverly toward her room on the right and me in the direction of some narrow, wooden stairs at the end of the entry hall. "Be careful now, Warren. They're steep." I knew she was going to say that. Our voices echoed in that empty house with no carpet covering the wooden floors. Like the apartment, the place had that faint odor of some other family who didn't change their underwear often enough, but Mom would take care of that soon.

I was struggling to get up to my hideaway as fast as I could, so that my folks wouldn't think it was too much for me and change their minds about letting me have the attic. My crutch was in my left armpit, and my right hand was on the railing, which allowed me to pull myself up, while I would hop to the next step on my good, right leg.

"You can still change your mind about the attic, Buddy!" Dad had watched me from the bottom of the steps.

"No soap."

I flung the crutch up in the air, over the stairwell railing and into my room. I used both arms to raise myself to each new level the rest of the way, unencumbered. I had already streamlined this stupid task on the first try and was becoming more and more excited with each tread. Three more hops, and I was there in my *attic*. It was HUGE! It was COOL! It was MINE! And I was pooped.

My dad came up after he saw that I had successfully conquered the climb. "Whattya think?" I was too busy taking it all in. It had a peaked ceiling with big, old wood beams, a rough, wood floor and windows at each end. It was kind of crude and musty smelling, but I didn't care. It was real perfect for me and my stuff. Dad had said something about some insulation and paneling for the sides, but I was already seeing my airplanes hanging from those big beams.

"When's the van getting here, Dad?"

"Soon, Buddy Boy. Wait 'till you hear it RAIN up here, Rastus!"

At that minute, there was no time for sad thoughts and fears. I was already deciding where my bed would be, and I looked forward to showing my buddies my room. Then, I remembered that I didn't have any buddies.

My sis hadn't let the movers pack her radio back in Lexington. She had taken it to the apartment, and now had it playing music … something about the Hucklebuck. I saw the van slowly pull up to the curb in front, because I had a bead on the world from my front window. Before long, there was a ramp sticking out of the back of the truck, and furniture and boxes were being paraded to the front door. I kept wondering when I would recognize some stuff of mine. There was the shiny, chrome kitchen set, my parents' bedroom set, the Atwater Kent radio, my sister's furniture, boxes, the lawn mower and, finally, my best treasure … my **Schwinn Black Phantom with balloon tires, chrome fenders, horn, tank, whitewalls, head and tail lights and spring fork, deluxe saddle.** All my pals were wishing for that same bike, and we could recite that spiel without taking one breath. I had earned half the money to pay for it by delivering papers; Dad paid the other half. But, as I watched it roll down that ramp, I just wanted to kick it and throw it in front of a train. I hated the thought of never riding it again. I saw Dad lovingly push it up the driveway toward the garage in the back. He had a hopeful and determined look in his eyes, like he was thinking, *someday.*

My spirits lifted a little when I finally saw my own bed.

"Up there." Dad said to the men and pointed toward my window, which I had struggled to open, so I could prop my elbows on the sill and watch the parade. In due time, my bookcase, my desk and chest of drawers (I pronounced it *chesterdoors*) were shouldered up the steps and thumped down on the floor in the middle of the room.

While beds were being put up and mattresses were flung onto the tops of them, Mom was at the grocery store. In a little while we had the basics of every boy's rations ... bread, American cheese, peanut butter, milk, apples, tomato soup, eggs, Post Toasties, grape jelly and butter, along with some other stuff Mom needed. These were the things that were important to me. Early in the afternoon, we were sitting at the kitchen table smacking our lips, as we ate peanut butter and jelly sandwiches and milk to wash them down, the best feast ever. Mom had started a pot of coffee that was percolating on the stove. "It makes it seem like home." Mom had said. I noticed a roll of toilet paper had miraculously appeared in the bathroom when I made my pit stop before the trip back up to my attic.

We all spent the afternoon opening up and putting away. I had clumped up the stairs to my room, once again, and looked at my important belongings and treasures. I remember shoving my bed into at least five different strategic places, settling on the front end of the bedroom, but sideways, by the east window. I could look at the sky from my bed and put my pillow on the sill in the summer when it was hot at night. It wasn't easy, I remember, due to the fact that I was hopping on one leg doing this labor. I got easily winded in those early days after the polio. I sat on my twin bed, going through a box that held my tin soldiers, marbles, baseball cards, my St. Louis Cardinals pennant, my Tom Mix Sliding Whistle Ring, my slinky, my yo yo, my Rawlings mitt that Dad gave me on my last birthday, a baseball and a lot of other stuff. When I first opened the box, it kind of smelled of sweat, leather and my old room back in Lexington. It was as if some of that same air traveled with the box in the van and was set free when I opened it. It was like seeing old friends again, and it made me feel good.

After the movers were gone, and Mom had located a pot and a pan, we had grilled cheese sandwiches and tomato soup. My mother knew how to make the house feel more like home. "I saw a Roberts Dairy truck go by today! We'll have to get ourselves on the route." Later on, we also had the Omar Man, who had bread and sweet rolls. I loved it when she would flag down that big, square truck, because it meant we would have cinnamon buns for breakfast.

It felt strange in bed in my new attic, where nothing was where it was supposed to be. I would close my eyes and try to pretend I was back in my old room, then open my eyes again and surprise myself, because I would be looking at something strange and forgetting what direction I was facing. It was kind of a rush, that dumb, silly game.

We had all gone to bed early, and it wasn't long before the house was quiet. A different quiet. Earlier, Mom and Dad had gotten on both sides of my bed to put on the sheets and blankets. I remember my mother asking me if I had gone to the bathroom. She was worried about my negotiation of the stairs during the night if I had to go. Our only bathroom was located on the first floor between the two bedrooms just off the entry hall. I assured her that I had. My folks pulled the blankets up to my chin. Mom kissed my nose, and Dad ruffled my hair and kissed my head. "Good night, Rastus." Sometimes he called me that. I don't know why. It felt good. I didn't hear all of those new sounds that are part of a new house, because I was dead asleep before I could listen very long. It was a good thing. If I had stayed awake for any length of time, I might have cried a little bit, I think.

◆   ◆   ◆

I woke up disoriented, because that little game of mine was still going on in the morning. I was startled when my eyes didn't see what they expected to see. The ceiling looked so high, and the bright sun was streaming into my eyes through that new east window. I didn't have a real door like the one at the old house, only a stair rail and the steps down to the hallway by the kitchen, where Mom was running water to make coffee again. That running faucet made me suddenly realize how bad I had to pee. I just couldn't have an *accident* up here, because I was sure I would be demoted to the downstairs, and Beverly would fly up here in victory, two steps at a time. Like hell, she would.

I have this terrible memory of rolling to the edge of the bed, grabbing my crutch and thumping to the stair's edge with my free hand holding my penis. I just knew I couldn't get to the bathroom in time. In a panic, I flung that crutch down the stairs. Still holding my whank, I dropped to a sitting position on the top step. I was covered with bruises the next day after that bumpy ride I took sliding down the stairs, holding my body stiff like a sled. That whole descent took less than four seconds of my precious time. Hearing my crutch stuttering its way down the steps, followed by me riding my butt down that bumpy slide with my metal leg brace clunking along ahead of me, Mom came racing into the hall. "WARREN!" I'll never forget the terrified look in Mom's wide eyes when she found me flat on my back with my head on the bottom step.

"Pull me up, Mom! I gotta take a whiz! REAL BAD!"

I stood in blessed relief, facing the throne in my flannel pajamas with cowboys all over them. It was a trauma I'll never forget, and Mom never said a word to anybody else about it, nor did she question my ability to occupy that upstairs castle. I loved my mom.

◆   ◆   ◆

Most folks my age would have trouble remembering the details of a move from one town to another, long ago, when they were only ten years old. But a life-changing monster had gotten hold of me, and that monster's name was POLIO. That's what made that move so permanently stored in my brain. Life had been all about me and my needs. Looking back on it, I know it had to be hard on Beverly, but what ten-year-old boy would have a whole lot of empathy for a big sister?

It wasn't by osmosis that our new house became home. It was a result of Mom's hard work and Dad's dependability. I had most of my stuff where I wanted it, and the beams of my roof were alive with hanging airplanes that were always slightly in motion, depending on my activities and the breeze that might come in through the windows. I had finally gotten my own radio out of some box, and I could listen to the ball games. The Tom Mix Show, the Creaking Door and Inner Sanctum were some of my favorites … and I didn't go outside. Not ever. The folks worried and fretted a lot and were always prodding me to get some air and maybe meet a friend. It would be "just what the doctor ordered!" My mom would say. My idea of living in the wild with wolves and deer had faded. I had my attic. I dreaded the end of the summer when school would start, and Mom would have to deliver me and pick me up, when everyone else would be walking those few blocks. I even thought of asking the school janitor to let me eat with him down in the furnace room, rather than face all of those mean kids that probably would laugh at me or ignore me, altogether. I knew that I would be known as THAT KID WITH THE CRUTCH AND THE BRACE. I even fantasized the school getting struck by lightening and burning to the ground before September.

I had one of those round mirrors hanging on a hook over my desk, and on a particularly boring day, I decided to take it down when the sun was fairly high in the sky. If I faced the mirror out my east window, the sun would bounce off it and put stuff in a very bright spotlight. I shined it on the mailman one time when he was coming up our front walk. He squinted and looked up at me. "Don't blind me, Roger Dodger!" On another day, I was leap-frogging that bright beam along the windows of the houses across the street. All of a sudden, I was blinded by a lightening-like flash coming from a yard that was two doors down on the other side of the street. Another mirror? The beam swiped across my eyes three times. I swiped mine back at the shooter three times. When he put his mirror down, I saw a kid with chalk white hair and a pink face, shading his eyes from the sun and looking up at me. Crummy copycat. Another beamshooter had sneaked into my private little world.

WARREN'S HOUSE

4

RAIN CHECK FOR WENDY

I'm barefoot in my robe trying to hop my way down the driveway without touching my feet to the cold, wet cement. It's kind of like Jack Nicholson's little dance of avoiding the cracks in AS GOOD AS IT GETS. It's cloudy and raining, blowing that bone-chilling, early spring, Nebraska wind out of the northwest. The guy who delivers the Sunday paper has flung the World Herald about twenty feet short of my covered front porch. I guess it has to do with the fact that the Sunday bundle with all of the ads weighs about thirty pounds. The week day delivery person puts it right by the door. I'm such a dumb shit going out there without my shoes on.

My Sundays are fairly well planned, usually. Coffee is first on the list after the bathroom, and it's now gurgling and dripping. Barnabus has crunched his way through the top layer of his Cat Chow and is now cleaning his privates on the table. "Off!" I'm spreading the paper out onto the kitchen table, downing my morning pills with my juice, pouring myself a cup of coffee, crunching my peanut butter toast, reading the paper and cussing at the idiots who are trying to run the country. I voted, but it didn't help.

I'll be meeting Wendy and Bernie at Super Duper Buffet at one. It's our ritual on Sundays. I wish she would find someone. She knows I'm there if she needs anything, and I would walk through hell fire for her and Bernie. I adore her and my grandson, but they need more than an old man who can fish with Bernie and take them out to eat. I can't fill that gap of the other more energetic stuff they're missing. Could be, that Wendy doesn't fill me in on every aspect of her life, however. I take some comfort in thinking that her social life is much more than just old, tired me.

Wendy went back to college after the Ass Hole left her. She's a legal secretary now. My grandson is in special school. Eventually, he will be placed in an adult, independent living center that is supervised, and he may be able to do a simple job. He is a Down's syndrome child. I'm anxious for the weather to get warmer, and we can go fishing again. I gave him his own tackle box and rod and reel a couple of years ago. You should have seen his face light up when I took him to Canfield's for that purchase. His little slanted, blue eyes were shining, and a wide, beefy smile was on his mouth. His thick little tongue was sticking out over his lower lip. He is such a joy, and has a sweet disposition. Once in a while, he acts out or throws a little tantrum about something. This makes it hard on Wendy, now that he has grown into a larger kid with some weight on him. Sometimes, I allow myself to imagine what Bernie would be like if he weren't … then I feel guilty. I'm human.

I'm standing in front of the bathroom mirror, contemplating the six or seven white hairs on my chest and fixing to take a shower, when the phone rings. It's Wendy.

"Hi, Daddy. I dote thik its godda work out today. I habba really bad code." I hear her blow her nose.

"Awe, that's awful! What about my little Trooper? Can I come get him and the two of us can go anyway?"

"Hate to tell you, Dad, but his dose is ruddig too."

"The heck, you say."

As a Down's syndrome child, Bernie is more prone to respiratory problems than other kids. That damned forty seventh chromosome. We're grateful that he has been healthy enough to participate in Special Olympics. Wendy and I always cheer him on and hug him afterward. That physical activity helps keep Trooper's weight down, too.

I offered to deliver some take-out from somewhere, but Wendy begged off. "I dote want to expose you, Dad. Deither of us is very hugry eddyway. I thik it's godda be oatbeal and puddig."

We said our goodbyes with promises to catch up later, and as usual, when there is a plague, I tell them to drink lots of liquids.

Feeling cold from simply talking to Wendy, I'm jumping into a hot shower. My jeans, flannel shirt, warm socks and slippers wait for me on the bed. I'm kicking the thermostat up another notch and pouring another cup of coffee, while I mentally plan my gear for the upcoming caper with Whitey. This damn rain could put a hold on the whole plan, or if Whitey and I were real tough, the rain could work to our advantage and be great cover. Even the dumb shits who burglarize people's houses wait for better weather than this. But, when I think of Wendy, abandoned in K.C. with a retarded son, I get madder than hell all over again, and I'm rarin' to go, regardless of the weather. The phone rings … Whitey.

"What … you're not in church?"

"No. Got your gear in the pickup?"

"Not yet. Thought you'd probably go yella on me."

"Not a chance. When you pickin' me up?"

"Two AM." Click. Typical Whitey.

5

IF YOU CAN'T BEAT 'EM, JOIN 'EM

Back at the house in Florence, it was several days before I was forced into a meeting with that white-haired kid. I was still holding my ground about staying to myself, except for my family. Before polio knocked me out of commission, I was right in the middle of a swell gang of pals out in Lexington. We played ball. We *lived* to play ball! I was shortstop, and a damn good one, too. I could move fast and react with one second of time to cover in a steal attempt or throw out a fast runner at first. Shortstop was a big time defensive position, because there were more right-handed hitters who put the ball between second and third. Dad would always be up for a game of catch. He would hit grounders to me, and I got so I could really dig 'em out of the dirt, but that backhand catch gave me the most trouble. Dad was always coaching me. *"Gotta have a good glove, good range and a strong arm."* I remember how sore my palm got when Dad took a notion to fire several hot ones in to test my toughness. My pals and I played ball during school recess when the weather cooperated; we played after school and all summer long. I can still see that mitt hanging on the handlebars of my bike, always ready for a game. I loved the feel of that mitt and would spend hours rubbing saddle soap into the leather and slapping the ball into the pocket while the game was on the radio. I had written WARREN HEARST in ink on the inside. On the pocket it said **Willie Mays** in fancy writing. It was a part of me, but now, that mitt was down in the bottom of my *chesterdoors* with my underwear.

My mother was getting more and more frustrated, because I refused to go outside and talk to that little kid with the mirror. "He looks to be about your age, Warren!" I was happy to settle for the "beamshooter" stuff, and I wanted my Mom to quit twisting my arm about talking to that creepy little kid.

On this particular day, and I'll never forget it, I was sitting on my bed fiddling around with my cars. I could hear the living room radio. Mom had the Hartz Mountain Canaries on. I wasn't much for that program. It was nothing but a bunch of violins playing, accompanied by a flock of birds, singing their heads off. (I'm off the subject, again.)

I'm sure my face must have been all screwed up, as I made shifting noises for my cars. ERRR, ERRR, ERRR. Each time, the sound was subtly different, depending on what gear it represented. That would be followed by hawking, throat noises that depicted killer crashes. I was too absorbed with this activity to notice that I had company.

"Hey!" Someone barked over the Hartz Mountain Canaries. I think I must have jumped a foot in the air, and the cars I had in my hands went flying skyward, hitting the high ceiling and falling back down. One hit me right smack on the head, and I grabbed my blanket to cover my leg brace. I wanted to crawl clear under the covers. The kid's fluorescent, white head glowed in the sun light that streamed in through my window, and I could see straight into his brain through his pink, transparent eyes. They glowed like a cat's eyes at night. It was several seconds before I could say anything to this intruder who stood right there in my private room, looking like a creature from Mars. I was mad as hell at my mom who had the nerve to let anybody come up *MY* stairs, *uninvited.*

"Hey, kid! You didn't beam me this morning. How come?"

I just stammered. My voice was shaking, and words wouldn't come out. I was so embarrassed, shocked and mad all at the same time. My anger finally kicked in, and I remember tearing into him with those words that had been stuck down in my throat.

"What are you doin' up here, CREEP? Did my Mom let you in? I didn't know we had a stupid BEAMIN' SCHEDULE, for cryin' out loud!

"I'm Whitey. My real name is Duane, but they call me Whitey ... know why?"

"Yeah, I can see why. I'd be real dumb if I couldn't."

"Wanna meet my dog?"

"No. 'Cause I'm not plannin' on goin' anywhere."

"What's this?" He grabbed my crutch from the bed and started swinging it around and pretending it was a ball bat.

"Gimme it!" I lunged forward and grabbed the top end. Whitey stubbornly hung on with those pink eyes glaring at me and smiling. I didn't think it was a very fair competition. He started taking little steps backward toward the stairs. I was off the bed by now, hopping on one leg and holding onto my end of the crutch for dear life.

"Wanna play tug of war with me, Kid?" He was giggling, and I hated him for that.

I was trying to hop and keep my balance, but it wasn't long before I fell forward, still holding on to my crutch in a death grip. I was being tugged toward the steps on my belly, and Whitey was starting to back down the long flight of stairs. Some of my former scrappiness was coming out. With a thud, I was down one step, and the kid kept on snickering at me. I was so mad, I could have killed him. After about twelve bumps, I was on the floor at the bottom of the steps in a humiliated heap. I was remembering the last time I thumped down those stairs.

"You dumb piece of crap, gimme my crutch!" I know the cords in my neck were standing out. Beverly always told me that's what happened when I got real mad and threw a fit when she took a notion to tease me.

"Here you go, kid." The little twerp finally let go.

Then my Mom came around the corner and gave Whitey a look, as if the two of them had a big conspiracy going. She opened the back door, and there was a big explosion, as this gigantic, yellow mutt raced in with his toenails clipping across the linoleum and his tongue hanging out. He had a dumb, dog smile on his face, as he leaped right on top of me, burrowing his wet nose under my chin, in my ears and armpits. He was snarling and whuffling and French kissing my mouth and my eyes and my nostrils. By now, even though I was trying my darndest to stay mad, I was starting to giggle, right along with Whitey and my

Mom. Two minutes later, that dumb mutt was sitting under the kitchen table breathing warm dog breath into my crotch, while Whitey and I were slugging down milk and chomping on ginger snaps.

"His name is Samson. I think he kinda likes you, Pal."

6

WHAT'S COOKIN'?

It's suppertime, Monday. I'm awake, because Barnabus has made it his business to bug me. It's unusual for me to be asleep all afternoon, ruining a cat's schedule. When Barnabus misses his rituals that depend on yours truly, I hear about it, which is why I'm awake. Barnabus is standing on the place where my six-pack abs would be if I had any. He's letting his heft sink into a cat nap position on my chest with four paws curled under him. Just as my eyes are beginning to close again for one last doze in the sack, Barnabus thinks it is a perfect time for the old padding routine. Left, Right, Left, Right … on my mouth, like a kitten, nursing and massaging mama's teat. His stiff whiskers are now needling my lips, and cat nostrils are examining my nose hairs. I sneeze, and Barnabus springs from my stomach to the foot of the bed, honoring me with a raised tail and a rock star view of his back door. I hear the thud when his feet hit the floor, and I know he is on his way to the kitchen, where he'll be sitting disgustedly by his dish. Old Barnabus was really Gwen's kitty, but I have moved up in his eyes since her death. I am now the one being used. We're sharing our golden years together. I don't know whose years are the most golden.

I had stayed up past midnight, quite a feat for me, since I'm usually gone to dreamland before ten thirty these days. I did this in order to facilitate a nap today. You see, I'm not used to sleeping while the sun shines, so I need to be tired in order to do so, since Whitey and I will be up most of the night.

I don't know how this cat knows I'm an hour late with his supper. As the Friskies are rattling into his dish, I can hear the March wind whipping around the eves. Sounds damn cold. The street looks dry, mercifully. Twenty four hours has made a difference in the weather. That's Nebraska for you.

I'm selecting one of my stash of frozen dinners with my eyes shut. Turns out, it is roasted chicken with whipped potatoes and a *moist, dark chocolate brownie.* I like to surprise myself. I buy these culinary wonders ten at a time. The girl at the checkout always teases me.

"Looks like you're having another dinner party tonight."

"You betcha." It's a ritual. Her name is Susie, and she has long, blond hair down to her ... well, enough of that. I like her. She calls me Dudley.

I'm opening the cardboard box, slitting the protective film and slipping it into the zapper. Barnabus is sitting on my placemat licking his butt, and the phone is ringing. It's Whitey.

"Just callin' to confirm that we have a *go,* Buddy Boy. I got all my stuff in the pickup and my gear laid out. Dress in layers. Colder'n hell out there."

"I hear ya."

"I'm takin' Connie out for a steak. Bribery for her not tellin' anybody about the project." I hadn't thought about Connie knowing. Of course, she would be suspicious when her husband got up in the middle of the night and took off.

"Had to tell her. Nothin' else I could do, although she did make a comment, that if I was tellin' her lies, I ought to be able to do better than that. Like I said, I'll pick you up at two AM, and it won't take long to load your stuff. Connie's gonna make us up some sandwiches and a thermos of coffee, and I got us some beer. You OK with all this?"

"Yep, I am. You have good wife. Do you know that?"

"I know. Later." Click.

7

THE PARTY'S OVER

When I first arrived in Florence in '49, I had my mind made up that nothing was going to go right. Everybody would have stuff going on but me. My sister, at age sixteen, would find friends. Beverly was very pretty and outgoing. She met some girls immediately, and simply by accident, as it turned out. There was a Reed's Ice Cream stand over on Thirtieth Street about two blocks from our house, and on that particular Saturday in June, Beverly decided she couldn't survive another minute without a clown sundae. As luck would have it, two other girls were hanging around there, licking their ten-cent ice cream cones. Reed's ice cream used to come packed in long cylinders. If you wanted a five-cent cone, they would cut off two or three inches and set it into the little cake cup. Ten cents would get you about five inches. Anyway, a little while later, here they came. All three of 'em. My sis had obviously changed her mind about stuffing herself with the clown sundae, because she was slurping on the smaller choice of a cone.

I remember them coming in the front door, giggling, and the two new friends were telling Beverly all about the boys at school. My sister showed them her bedroom with the new pink, flowered curtains and matching bedspread from the Sears Catalog. I heard Beverly tell them that Mom had painted the walls herself. They were pink, too. It kind of made my stomach lurch. Not just the color pink, but the fact that Beverly was already in the thick of things and moving on with new friends. I figured she wouldn't be paying quite as much attention to me when there were girls to talk to, and boys wouldn't be too far behind.

My big event for that day was to spend some time with Dad down in the basement, helping him set up his ham radio set. Once in a while, he would let me talk into the clumpy microphone, and I got to use his call letters, KXJZ. We would contact people all over the world. Dad had a big bulletin board, and we were going to mount it on the wall, so that he could post all of the QSL calling cards from his contacts. I planned to have my own ham radio someday when I got big. Dad had one in the car, too. I don't remember exactly at what age the desire for one faded. But I need to get back to the subject.

The day I met Whitey and was pulled down the steps and mauled by his dog was just the beginning of some big changes in my drab life. Every time I thought I couldn't do something, Whitey ignored that idea.

One morning, I looked out my east window and saw Whitey and his dog, Samson, lounging in the grass. A bike was lying on its side. Samson had a big ball with no air in it clamped in his teeth. I remember feeling nervous about what Whitey might have up his sleeve.

"Whattya doin' down there? I ain't even had breakfast yet!" I yelled from my window.

"Your dad was just leavin' for work, and he tossed me a whole pack of Yucatan gum, as he was backin' the car out of the driveway! You jealous, Thumper Boy?"

"Go jump off a cliff."

"Can't do that, *Warren*. Your mom invited me in for breakfast."

"Criminey." Whitey always used my real name when he wanted to get at me. He would say it real whiney like. I actually liked THUMPER better, even though it referred to my brace and my crutch. I got the feeling that there was another WHITEY-MOM CONSPIRACY in the works.

I had developed a new, streamlined style of descending the stairs. My good leg was getting stronger, because it just plain had to. I would grab the railing down as far as I could reach, then put my crutch down three steps ahead of myself. Then I would hop down to that third step, (skipping two) and go on like that to the bottom. I didn't get any bruises with this method, and it was much less painful than the old toboggan style. Dad had installed a second railing so that I had one on both sides of the stairs. Lucky me, to have a dad like that.

I was already dressed before the appearance of Whitey, luckily. It was the additional task of putting on the brace that disgusted me. I hopped down the steps, peed, wet my tooth brush (without actually brushing my teeth) and hobbled into the kitchen to find Whitey sitting in front of a bowl of cereal. He's an early bird. Samson was parked under the table with his chin in Whitey's lap. Mom poured me my cereal and milk, and when she turned her back on me to put the milk away, I dumped a whole bunch of sugar on top.

"How come you're up so *early?*" I said to Whitey.

I remember many of these snippets of conversations from those days, because they lead up to some very traumatic events that happened that summer.

"Been waitin' for *you.*" Whitey spooned some sugar into his palm and stuck his tongue into it. He always did stuff like that, as if it were perfectly normal and reasonable. I wouldn't have tried that in front of my mom.

"Criminey." I finished my Toasties and drank the rest of the very sweet milk in the bottom. Whitey just smirked at me with his chin in his palms and his elbows on the table.

"Nice day out." Mom smiled at my friend. It was that same smile she used on that day Whitey made me crash to the bottom of my stairs on my stomach in that tug of war with my stupid crutch.

"Yeah, you need some sunshine, THUMPER! I wanna show you somethin'!" I knew he was probably setting me up for something, that little creep. Whitey was sly like a fox. We went out and sat on the porch swing, and Whitey pulled a Duncan yo yo out of his jeans pocket. I started to tell him that I had a yo yo upstairs, but rather than let me escape into the protection of my house, he kept talking and pulled out another yo yo for me. Said everybody brought one to school all the time. This strategy lured me off the porch to the front yard, where Whitey showed me his expertise at WALK THE DOG, ROCK THE BABY, and AROUND THE WORLD. I knew those tricks, but was never very good at them.

I had been leaning on my crutch during those maneuvers with the Duncans, and I finally let myself fall into the grass. Polio had knocked the starch out of me, and I got tired real fast in those days. I just lay there looking up at the blue sky, smelling the fresh air. Whitey flopped down too, and Samson wedged himself between us. I got a token lick on my ear.

Then, there was that day Whitey showed up with his bike again. Whitey lived only a couple of houses down on the other side of the street and didn't need transportation, but in those days, a kid's bike was part of him. I was lonesome as hell for my Black Phantom that hung in the dark from a big hook in the garage. I hadn't thrown it in front of a train, after all. Maybe there was a silent, eternal hope in my young soul.

"Be right back." Whitey raced into my house. He was starting to act right at home here, and I asked him where he was going. He was already on his mission and ignored me. When he showed up again, he leaped from the porch and almost *floated* in slow motion to the sidewalk without touching the wooden steps. My ball glove, which hadn't seen sunshine since I came down with polio, was dangling from his hand.

"What are you doin' with my glove?" I was irritated that he had been in my underwear drawer without my permission. I wondered how he even knew where to look.

"Your mom told me it was OK. Come over here." He hung my glove on the handle bar next to his. Samson had the ball in his mouth.

Once again, I was the object of a conspiracy and madder than hell at my mom.

"I ain't goin' NOWHERE!" Those cords in my neck must have been really bulging.

"Hop over here, and leave that crummy crutch in the yard, or I'm ridin' off with your mitt!"

"The HELL you are!" I took several struggling hops at him with my eyes shooting death rays. About that time, I lost my balance and fell on my butt. Whitey got me in a bear hug from behind and hefted me by the waist onto the seat of his bike, which was waiting at a funny angle on its stand. It couldn't have been easy for Whitey with me flailing around, but I wound up on that seat anyway. In seconds, we were sailing down the street. Samson loped along behind us with the ball in his teeth. His chops were flapping up and down as he galloped. Whitey was standing up, peddling like hell, and I was cussing a blue streak with my fingers hooked into his belt, nearly cutting off the circulation in my hands. After a few more seconds, it came to me that I was having a real cool time doing something fast and *dangerous*. Whitey was strong.

By this time, I was laughing and whooping it up, and we were heading straight toward the curb by the school playground. I closed my eyes real tight, because I was bracing myself for a catastrophe. I never even felt the crash I was bracing myself for, only a slight … *lift*. The next thing I knew, the tires were scrunching into the gravel on the BLOOM ELEMENTARY playground. The bike slid to a fishtail stop, and Whitey awkwardly dismounted, swiping the kickstand. He grabbed my waist and pulled me off, as the bike fell over. Kickstands don't do too well in gravel. They just sink. That two-wheeler just lay there like a tired dog, and I wanted to do the same thing, believe you me.

I was weak and shaking from the shock of being kidnapped and whisked away from the safety of my house. Just as I was beginning to think I couldn't stand there any longer, hopping on one leg, Whitey handed me my mitt. "Stand right there, Thumper." He tossed me the ball, which deflected off my glove and into the air. I hopped to position and managed to snag it with my right hand and triumphantly slap it into the pocket. I lost my balance and fell with a crunch into the gravel. But I hadn't dropped the ball!

"You ain't a lost cause yet!" Whitey ran out to the field.

"Fire it in here!" He was standing with his legs spread, knees bent, and his glove was right in front of his face with his pink eyes staring just over the top of it. By this time, the leg I was depending on was rapidly beginning to weaken. I flung the ball in his general direction, which wasn't easy, balancing on one leg. Whitey reached way out to the side and retrieved it.

"Not bad for a crip!" He fired it right back at my face. My natural reflex was still in tact, and my mitt was exactly in front of my nose when that flying missile hit the pocket. After a few seconds of this, my leg failed me. I sank to the ground, lying flat on my back and looking at the sky. Samson, who had been running back and forth between us, trotted over and collapsed to the ground next to me.

His chin was on my stomach, and I could feel his drool coming through my shirt. Whitey came and flopped down, too. We looked at the blue sky and the clouds, and for the first time since I moved to Florence, life seemed almost good.

"That was kinda fun."

"You needed that, Pal."

We talked for a while about the stuff ten-year-old boys talked about back in 1949. Box hockey in the park, baseball and the new stadium that was being built, flying saucers at Roswell and BLOOM ELEMENTARY, where I would be going in the fall. *If I didn't become a hermit.* I told Whitey about my old school in Lexington and how I played shortstop before I got sick.

Suddenly, Samson was on his feet, and his fur stiffened up on his back. He bared his teeth, and a sound like an engine idling came from deep in his throat. He had that wild dog smile with chops curled up on the side and wicked incisors showing. His eyes were fixed on the jungle gym by the northwest corner of the school building, as three mean looking hoods were kicking gravel and scuffing their way toward us. They had cigarettes and looked real tough. I couldn't get up to a standing position without help, and helpless is what I was. "Criminey, who are *they?*" I thought I would probably get beat up, but good, and wet my pants on top of it, I was so scared.

"They're eighth graders, and everybody knows 'em. Eddy, Richie, and Gordon are their names, but everybody calls 'em Spider, Rat and Weasel. Don't do nothin'. Just sit still. Stay, Samson." I could smell that odor that dogs give out when there is danger. There is no smell like it. I wondered if maybe I was the one causing that stink.

I was beginning to worry about what Mom and Dad would do if I never showed up back home. I wished I could make my brace disappear. I wished I had my Schwinn Black Phantom and could burn out, shooting the gravel back in their faces as I raced away. But I couldn't race away. I couldn't even stand up by myself.

"Who's your pal with the tin leg, COTTON HEAD?" Spider was chunking his engineer boot in the gravel, which was shooting up in the air and hitting me in the face and pinging off my leg brace. I just sat there shaking with my hands digging at the gravel. Rat and Weasel snickered and mimicked, "Yeah, who's your pal with the tin leg, COTTON HEAD?" It didn't take me long to know who the dumb ones were and who the leader was.

"Who wants to know?" Whitey stood up in defiance. I could see the muscles in his jaw working as he chewed his gum faster and harder. My pal was standing his ground with his hand on Samson's head. The dog's throat was rumbling again, and he was in that *stance* with his head and tail lowered. I remember how wild his eyes looked, and the fur along his spine was *up*.

"Take care of that dumb dog." Spider elbowed Weasel, who looked at his pals like they had rocks in their heads. Weasel, with the lowest intelligence, was probably the one who was dumb enough to attempt taking on the mutt. I remember Weasel's bulky body edging closer and closer to Samson, his beefy hands ready to grab Man's Best Friend around the neck. Whitey stood away from his dog at that time, knowing that Samson could handle the Weasel. With a snoring intake of breath, a snarl and the snapping of sharp incisors, Samson ripped a permanent, scar-colored tattoo on Weasel's fat forearm.

"I don't think my little doggie likes you."

"Get him off me!" Samson went for his leg, puncturing the thigh in several places. Weasel fell on his backside and curled up in a ball with his arms over his head, while Rat and Spider backed way off with their tough act all gone.

"Go sit by Warren, Samson."

Miserable whimpering didn't make that Weasel guy look so tough anymore. After Samson lifted his leg, relieving himself on Weasel's head, he calmly ambled over to me and sat, as if nothing had happened.

"Next time I see that dog, I'm gonna shoot him." Weasel sobbed, rocking back and forth, as he held his bleeding leg.

"Yeah, shoot him." Rat always was imitating. He had no ideas of his own, I guessed.

"You best be lookin' over your shoulder from now on, PINK EYES. And the crummy cripple, too! We're gonna go now, but we'll be back in a few minutes, and you better not be here!" They tried to look cool and tough pulling Weasel up off the ground. They sauntered away, looking cocky, but knowing they were out-done, embarrassed and scared spitless.

"You told *them*!" Rat had nothing else to say.

I was just starting to feel like we were out of the woods, when Whitey yelled at Weasel, who was still limping from a dog attack.

"Hey, Shit Face, whose the CRIP NOW?" Three goons spun around and were charging at us. I was preparing for my death, and I wanted to kill Whitey for risk-ing our lives with his big mouth. I couldn't figure out why Whitey had that kind of *NERVE* in the face of such danger. Samson stood like stone next to his master with his teeth bared and his throat motor in idle. I was glued to the ground, shak-ing and praying, as the three reached us, spraying the gravel once again as they skidded to a stop in front of us. Weasel stayed behind Rat and Spider, keeping a careful eye on Samson. Spider was still the leader.

"Weasel, you take little Tin Leg. Rat and I got Loud Mouth and Four Legs."

I started to scream and tried to scoot away from the big, dumb one, who grabbed my brace and began to pull me around in the sand. Rat pulled a knife and started for Samson, who went for another leg to chew on, but he yelped as Rat stabbed the muscle in hind leg. Samson leaped for Rat's neck, in spite of his injury. Spider had a wad of Whitey's T-shirt in his left hand, ready to punch him in the face, and maybe break Whitey's nose, if things worked out the way he wanted them to. But, things didn't work out the way the bullies thought they would.

The air seemed to change. There was no breeze, and my ears started to ring, as all the players in this killer game *froze* in mid-action. Even though I couldn't move, I could still see. Weasel's pudgy hands, gripped around my good leg, as he swung me around in a circle. I was off the ground, like "pause" on a DVD, just staring in horror at his angry face, which was also frozen on top of his statue-like body.

Samson was frozen in place on his way up to Rat's neck, while a knife, dripping dog blood, was clutched in a raised fist that was not moving, since Rat was not moving either.

Whitey's shirt was wadded up in Spider's hand. His arms hung limp with his palms forward. There was a smile on Whitey's face. All action had stopped when the neon pink beams shone from Whitey's riveting eyes, blinding Spider and paralyzing the fighters in this war zone. In the quiet horror and terror, Whitey spoke with his face a mere one inch from Spider's nose.

"You asked who my friend was. Well, the dog, floating over there by Rat, is Samson. He's a real special doggie, and I'm real angry about that knife cut in his rear. I can make that knife end up in your tum-tum, PAL. And, about my good buddy, (he's the one floating in front of Weasel) you'll be calling him Warren. *NOT* the kid with the tin leg. And, while I'm on the subject of Warren, you ain't seen nothin' of him yet, take it from me."

My mouth was open so far that a bird could have flown in there. I suddenly realized that nothing else in the neighborhood was moving, including birds. Whitey looked back at me and smiled. (He could do that, since he was sort of in charge.)

"Get a load of *this!*" He proudly surveyed the three helpless hoods and promptly allowed Samson and me to float gently to the ground. The mutt limped over next to me as close as he could get and began licking his wound.

Whitey returned his pink, beaming eyes to Spider's face. "Your Mommy wants you."

I could hear Spider whimpering as he was allowed to race away to parts unknown, not believing what he had just witnessed. He stopped long enough to vomit all over his engineer boots.

The next stop was Weasel, who had been spinning me around by one leg. He now hovered with one foot up and the other down in an awkward, frozen dance. His hands still were in the gripping position, as if my leg was still *in there*.

"Tell anybody about this, and you won't be able to control your bladder for the rest of your stupid life. You *get* it?" Whitey had sent number two of the three galloping away with both hands between his legs, and a dark, wet area was spreading down his trouser legs.

Whitey had saved Rat, who was still holding a knife with the blood of his beloved Samson dripping from it, for last.

"Spider and Weasel are on their way home to their mamas. I think you are in some trouble, too, but don't take my word for it." Whitey gently removed the sticky knife from Rat's hand and began sawing his way down the front of the rodent's striped shirt. When the galvanized Rat was at last allowed to race from the playground, the wind gusted and spat gravel into the crack of his bare behind. There weren't any pieces of clothing big enough for him to cover anything on his buck naked body.

I'm a peace loving guy, but in this day and age, I wish there was a little of this kind of magical justice, instead of cowardly guns.

SAMSON

8

FLOOZY OR FRIEND?

My folks are still alive. It amazes me. Dad is eighty five, and my mother is eighty seven. She used to get a kick out of telling everyone that she robbed the cradle. Dad wound up buying the garage and auto parts business where he worked when we moved to that house out in Florence.

My wife's parents had owned a lot of land in western Nebraska. They were weather beaten, hard working ranchers. They did well and managed their money well, but they died too early. It wasn't fair. When they were somewhere in their sixties, (Gwen and I were married and had had our daughter Wendy.) they were found in a creek bed in their overturned car in the middle of one of those heartland killer blizzards. They had gone to a Sunday night meeting at church in Lexington and never made it back out to the ranch. They weren't discovered until the next day. My wife, being their only child, inherited the place … land, cattle, house, buildings, equipment, gas well and all of their savings. I have to say, Gwen was the alpha female in our household, as far as the financial situation went. Gwen sold the whole package to a family with three boys, and then went to the bank. But I kept my business and stayed a respectable, contributing member of our household.

Anything we wanted, we could have, but we lived as we would have lived without that inheritance. A simple, loving and meaningful life. I thank God for Wendy and Bernie, but I still ache inside when I think about those years when I had my beautiful Gwen. I don't think I could ever marry again, even though Wendy has hinted at me about finding someone to travel with and enjoy a glass of wine with on the deck. *"I wish you would have some fun, Daddy!"* I can't picture myself getting taken in by anyone. I have to admit, I've had my "come-ons" as a single guy, but …

I'm digging out my dad's old thermal, lined jump suit from a chest in the basement, and it's lying on the bed. Barnabus is napping on it. If I survive the next few hours, I'll have one hell of a story to tell my folks. You can talk about the weather only just so long on a visit to Florence Hills Village assisted living center. Pops would love hearing an adventure for a change, if I come out of this thing alive. Mom won't care. Sadly, she doesn't have a clue who I am, now. I don't think it'll be too long before she'll leave Dad alone in the apartment. The Alzheimer unit is waiting. Those damn golden years have turned to tin for my folks.

When you're killin' time, it doesn't go too fast. All of the LAW AND ORDERS seem to melt into each other. Why I watch them, I don't know. None of the characters have a life outside of the office. SHARK, I can get into. It's ten PM. The local news is just starting with the announcement of the latest shooting near downtown Omaha, when my phone rings.

"Hi! Is this Warren?"

"Speaking." It's a woman.

"Oh, good! Hi, Cutie Pie! It's Petty. Remember? From Bucky's place? I feel funny calling you. I've never done this before! It's really not professional for me to be callin' customers, y'know."

What the HELL?

"I don't know if it's important, but I was bussin' up your table from breakfast this mornin' and found some hen scratchins on them PLACEMATS. Looked like maybe somethin' important, with all those lists and *TWO AM* written on one corner. Did you want me to hold on to 'em or throw 'em away, or what! I could bring 'em to your place if you need 'em right away … What are you two farts UP to, if you don't mind my askin'?"

I'm standing by the phone with my teeth clenched and my eyes pressed shut. There has been a leak at Bucky's place.

I'm explaining that it's all about a fishing trip and that the lists aren't important. I'm telling her that I have a bad habit of doodling when I'm talking to someone, and that the TWO AM doesn't mean anything. She can toss them.

"But I COULD bring 'em over!"

"Naw. It's OK. Thanks anyway, Petty."

"Well, all righty then. Bye bye." She sounds deflated.

"Yeah, thanks. Good night." *Hubba Hubba*

The news is over, and Leno is coming on. I'm rounding up my heavy socks and work boots with the steel toes, my long underwear, gloves, stocking cap and parka. I have located the tools, so now I'm wrapped up in my polar fleece robe that was a Christmas present from Wendy and Bernie, and I'm lounging in front of the TV. I got the alarm set for one AM, in case I should fall asleep in my recliner. Likely? Probably.

9

NOW I'VE SEEN EVERYTHING

I remember being a lot more cooperative coming home with Whitey than I was when I was first kidnapped from my front yard an hour ago. My knuckles were white, as I held on to Whitey's belt. I was sweating and almost ready to throw up because of what I saw on the playground. I wondered just *who was* this wonder kid who chose me to be his pal. We rolled into my driveway, followed by Samson, who dutifully had the ball in his mouth.

"You gonna be OK, THUMP?" Whitey's arms circled my waist and (gently this time) pulled me off the seat. He was curiously calm, and I didn't know how he could be so relaxed. But, as for me, my saliva glands were beginning to water, after which I heaved up my breakfast in the grass. I saw my mom on the front porch with a horrified look on her face.

"Oh, Good Lord!" She flew down the steps.

"I think Warren's had about enough for one day, Mrs. Hearst. Do you think we could have a little snack in your kitchen? He's probably hungry now."

I could tell that Mom was beginning to have second thoughts about her GET WARREN OUTSIDE IN THE FRESH AIR conspiracy with the little kid across the street.

Mom's voice wavered a little bit as she told Whitey it would be OK to have a snack and stay for just a few minutes. "After the snack, Warren should go up to his room and rest, Duane. But, thank you for spending time with him. You're a good friend, and Warren needs a friend."

I didn't want my "good friend" to go yet. I wanted some damn answers, and a cookie and a glass of milk wasn't going to hack it for me. Mom handed me my crutch from where we had left it before the hasty getaway, then Samson and the rest of us trudged into the noisy front hall. Beverly and her two new friends were squealing and giggling on top of the teen dance music on the radio in the bedroom. I asked Mom what was going on. "Oh, I suppose they're talking about hot rods, and bare midriffs or something. They were practicing the conga line and the jitterbug a while ago." Mom quickly got right back to the business of my health and my vomit in the front yard.

"Just what HAPPENED, Duane?" Mom called Whitey by his real name, usually. She had that DON'T MESS WITH ME look in her eyes, and I had my mouth open, but had nothing ready to say that she would believe. Then Whitey jumped in with his usual bull roar, and Mom just stood there with her hand on her hip. I was all ears.

"Mrs. Hearst, Warren just got scared 'cause he really didn't want to *go* in the first place, you know! And we, uh … kinda took a little *spill* in the gravel, just as we were leaving the school, and Warren got kinda upset. It wasn't really NOTHIN', Mrs. Hearst. I promise we won't go back in that gravel on the bike again! By the way, can Samson have a drink of water?"

Mom quietly took a medium mixing bowl out of the cupboard and filled it with water. She still didn't say anything, which I always hated, because I figured that she WOULD have plenty to say later on. Samson lapped at his water, slopping all over the floor about a foot in all directions, as Mom put the milk glasses in front of us. She had her tongue in the side of her cheek, and her mouth was all pursed. Mom glared at us, waiting for the rest of the story. A plate of homemade chocolate chip cookies was thumped down in front of us. Whitey couldn't stand the silence. "HONESTLY, Mrs. Hearst!" Whitey added, as if that would put an end to any questions about the playground caper.

"Eat your cookies, and then Warren goes up for a rest."

When the cookies were gone, Whitey wiped his mouth on his shirt, and, being VERY helpful, said he would assist me up the steps. Mom said that would be nice. "Five minutes."

We hit the top step to my room when I cut loose. "I gotta TALK to you, Whitey! Whattya mean scarin' the shit outta me like that? If you want my two cents worth, we're probably in big trouble with those tough guys. They're gonna *kill* us the next time they see us! How did you DO that creepy stuff? Did you come in on one of those flying saucers? Are you from MARS or something? Jeeze, you scared me! I'm almost *afraid* of you now! I hate to think of what would happen if you got mad at *me!*"

"Time's UP Duane!" We heard from the bottom of the steps.

"OK, Mrs. Hearst, I'm comin'! I'll see you tomorrow, Thump. Don't worry, those dinkum-gin-wits won't kill us or even remember anything, except to treat us *real good* from now on. Tomorrow we're gonna go meet Mr. Woodard. By the way, Thump, I would never ever ever hurt you, Pal. You're my best friend.

I was real confused, but I shouldn't have been. It was just like Whitey to leave me hanging up in the air like that. I rested a little easier after Whitey said he wouldn't ever hurt me.

"Who the heck is Mr. Woodard?"

"Tomorrow, *Warren.*" I heard the back door shut.

I sort of had to take a whiz, but not that bad. Going back downstairs and facing my mom didn't sound pleasant, so I squeezed my knees together and my eyes shut, hoping to get to sleep quickly. The last thing I remembered was my sister's radio playing "How Much is that Doggie in the Window."

Sometimes I kind of wished I had a dog.

10

IT'S NOT MY SCENE

I've been dozing, of course. I vaguely remember the weather report. Cloudy, winds, subsiding about midnight with the overnight low at forty degrees. No rain predicted. *Predicted.* That's the key word. I force Barnabus off my lap, and he follows me to the kitchen. Seven cat treats later, I'm making coffee with lead in it and hoping, since it is Monday, that Leno is exciting enough with his HEAD-LINES to keep me charged up for the caper. I have to kill three hours. I keep thinking about Petty from the cafe and wondering if I had put anything incriminating on that placemat. Maybe I should have told her I would come and pick it up, right then, just to shut her up and end the curiosity. Naw. That would place too much importance on the damn thing, and I have misgivings about being at her front door, anyway. Three hours is giving me too much time to think, making me paranoid. However, I still hope I didn't write the name WOODARD on that stupid placemat.

I have my SPECIAL OLYMPICS mug, and I'm pouring some of that stiff, Starbucks into it, when the phone rings. I know who it is.

"Did you tell that floozy from Bucky's anything?" *Busted.*

"What? I'm not worried about anything. There weren't any clues that she could really put together ... WERE there?"

"Not on YOURS, buddy boy. Mine had two AM on it and the name, WOO-DARD."

"Okay. She wanted to bring the stuff over to my place, I confess. I told her it was only some scribbles about plans for a fishing trip. No big deal about it."

47

"Well, she's here at my house right now, Thumper Boy! She and Connie are in the kitchen, and she's helping my wife make bologna sandwiches for the two of us. Connie let her in, and because of one too many glasses of vino at the steak house, my wife got a case of loose lips. You got any suggestions about how I can get rid of her?"

"Petty or your *wife?*"

"You're a riot."

"Well, we have a lot of time before we go. Have Connie make coffee and chit chat with Petty. She's probably a lonesome soul. She'll leave, sooner or later. Besides, you could just *whammy* her! Show your stuff! *Beam* her right on home. She won't remember a thing."

"This isn't a whammy situation, Buddy Boy. My last round of whammying was on the playground in 1949. Things have to be in crisis before I can use that power. Old Man Woodard told me the rules, and that's one of 'em. I'll figure it out and see you in about three hours. I gotta go. I'm on my cell phone in the front yard, and I'm freezin' my ass off. Click.

11

CABIN IN THE SKY

Getting back to my story ... when I woke up the next morning, I could hear Mom and Whitey talking in the kitchen. It was about eight AM, and I wondered how long my friend had been up and attem.

"The day's practically gone, Buddy Boy! Ain't it, Mrs. Hearst?" My mom smiled, as if nothing had happened yesterday. I wondered what additions to the sparse, playground tale Whitey had come up with and what psychological razzle-dazzle he had used on Mom.

"What do you want on your toast, Warren?" Mom pushed the handle down for my two slices. I told her I wanted butter, cinnamon and sugar. She had made cocoa, and Whitey was enjoying a cup. I could tell he had already had toast because of the crumbs on his red T-shirt. Samson was sprawled in the middle of the floor. "Duane has plans for a nice morning, if you're up to it." I just knew that she had been taken in by him again. I was getting nervous, because my friend's track record warranted it.

Mom poured my cocoa, while my toast toasted. I had been thinking about Whitey's family. I wondered why no one ever told *him* when to be home, and why he never talked about anyone at his house. Mom seemed to read my mind. "I would like to meet your mother, Duane. Maybe she could come over some-time for a cup of coffee."

"Grandma Mac lives with us and takes care of me during the day. Mom's at work at the beauty shop over on Thirtieth Street ... NORMA LOU'S SALON. She's the boss, because it's her own place."

Mom took the bull by the horns and asked, "Whitey ... Where's your father?"

"Gone."

Mom changed the subject. "Tell Warren about your exciting plans for this morning, Duane! I think you'll like this, Warren!" My pal had already made my life exciting enough, I thought.

"I brought the wagon, Thump. You're gonna ride like a king!"

"Ride WHERE?" I also wondered how FAR. I was always in the dark with Whitey.

Samson and I are gonna show you around the neighborhood and take you up to Mr. Woodard's place." When Whitey said, "Mr. Woodard's place", his eyes kind of changed a little bit. His eye balls were moving back and forth real fast, and they turned a more *intense* pink. Mom wasn't watching, thank God. I just knew she wouldn't let me go with him if she had seen that. She plunked a plate on the table with my two pieces of cinnamon toast and gave us each a glass of orange juice.

Beverly came bouncing into the kitchen. She had already been on the telephone with Patty and Virginia, who were just knocking at the door. Friends didn't live far away in 1949. "Mom, can I go to the movies with the girls tonight? We want to see LITTLE WOMEN and come back here for a slumber party. Please, please, PLEASE, Mom?" I hated that whiney stuff that Beverly pulled when she wanted something real bad.

Mom had a regular routine, when Beverly asked to go somewhere. "I suppose so, but we'll talk about it after Warren and Duane finish breakfast." She had that habit of making a person wait and suffer before she gave an answer. This would give my mom time to consider the negatives about a thing. The movie theater was only six blocks away from our house, and the girls would be walking. I knew Mom would have to go through the spiel about not getting into anybody's car and being careful about who my sister sat next to at the theater.

I wasn't born yet, but Beverly told me about the night my dad grabbed a man by his shirt, pulled him out of his theater seat and kicked his butt clear out onto the street. My folks had been sitting together by the aisle, and Beverly, who was only four, wanted to be "grown up" and sit *across* the aisle from them in the end seat. Dad had noticed that my sis kept hanging her feet out in the aisle, where someone could trip in the dark, so he scolded her about it. She told Dad that the man next to her kept touching her … in the wrong place. That man left the premises with a bloody nose and several teeth missing. There was no 911 in '49, but men sometimes used their fists to handle problems in those gentler days without assault weapons.

The real reason for the movie was the presence of boys, who would have spent the twelve cents to get in and find the girls. And there was the final mandate about coming right home afterward. "Stay together on your way home, girls. You remember that man who jumped out of a car and exposed himself to those two girls last week!" Mom always had warnings about all possible dangers. When the warnings started to come, Beverly knew the answer would probably be yes … they could go to the movie.

Beverly, Patty and Virginia were all squealing and huddling around the hall telephone, while Virginia and Patty took turns calling their mothers for permission.

The toast was gone, and Whitey wiped his face on his T-shirt, as usual. "Ready, Thump?"

My mom, being her usual self, warned us about cars and staying on the sidewalk and being home by lunch time. I took my crutch along, even though I would be riding in the coaster wagon most of the time, pulled by my friend. Whitey's plan was to take me on a long, overdue tour of our neighborhood in something other than our family car. At this point, and knowing Whitey as I now did, I wasn't worried about any tough guys who might give me a hard time. Soon, I was bumping along in the Radio Flyer over the cracks in the sidewalks.

Mom slipped us a quarter so we could stop at Spangler's Drug store for candy bars, and off we went. "We're gonna take the long way around so you can see where some people live, Thump." Samson jumped into the front of the wagon between my legs. I guessed that he must have been in the habit of doing that. "SAMSON! It's Thumper's turn, you lazy old mutt." Samson had that guilty dog look on his face and jumped out obediently. I thought it was kind of cozy in the wagon with the two of us.

We headed south down Bloom Street. I always wondered about that spooky house on the corner of my block. "Who lives *there?*" It was a huge, brick house, three stories high and surrounded with old trees and lots of shrubs. It sat at an angle on the corner lot with a long sidewalk up to the front steps. I remember two big cement lions, one on each side of the front door.

"Mrs. Kinsolving lives there, but nobody ever sees her. She's a witch. All the kids say so, and I kinda believe them. She's real old, at least 60. You should see the place at night! If you sneak around there with a flashlight, you can see cats in every window! Their eyes really light up. I been there lots of times, and it's true. All the bushes around there smell like cat pee, that's one bad thing. Everybody goes there on Halloween. The house is always dark, but she's there, all right. Somebody mows her grass, and once in a while you can see her in her big old black car, but not very often. We'll have to go there some night, Thump. Cool, huh?"

The thought went through my mind that the flashlight would do the same darn thing to Whitey's eyes that it does to the cats' eyes, but I kept my trap shut about that. "Does your mom know you do that?"

"Heck, no. I just sneak out my bedroom window after she goes to bed. She only caught me a couple of times. Grandma Mac can't hardly hear it thunder, and she's snoring in bed by eight thirty. I don't like it when she snores. It scares me a little bit, like if I went into her room while she was doing that, she would turn into a monster and leap out of her bed and come at me with pointy teeth and long, boney claws and ..."

Whitey trailed off that subject. I thought about how lucky I was to have some-body who would come and talk to me, even if it was in the middle of the night, when I needed to be comforted and told that somebody's snoring wasn't any-thing to be afraid of. That was one of the times I learned that not all kids had everything that I did.

We turned left and passed Stone Mortuary. "I've seen 'em take bodies in through the back door. I see lots of stuff." Samson watered a fire hydrant, and on we went. "There's Pete's bike shop. He's a great guy. He let's me go in there and look around all the time, and he'll fix something on my bike if it needs it. I don't have to pay him anything! Come on! I want you to meet him. Sometimes he blows warm smoke from his pipe into my ear when it aches."

Whitey beat me to the door, because my crutch got all tangled up with my leg brace, when I tried to get out of the stupid wagon. Samson was the first one in, and Whitey held the door for me. Pete came out of the back room where he fixed all the bicycles. I liked that smell of grease and gasoline and new rubber tires. Garage smells. Pete smoked a pipe, so that sweet smell was mixed in with the others in the workshop. I thought Pete must have been pretty old. He had this real devilish smile and little beady eyes with wrinkles in the corners. I liked him right away. "Who ya got there, Whitey m'boy?"

"This is Thump, I mean, Warren. He's new here, and I wanted him to see your shop."

He told me he was pleased to meet me. Whitey and I weaved our way between all the new bikes, and I noticed a Black Phantom, like mine. "You like that one, Bud?" I told Pete that I had one at home. I noticed him looking at my leg, but he didn't say anything about that. He did say he would like to see my bike sometime. "Bring yours in, and we'll give it a goin' over, how would that be?" I told him it was hanging out in the garage, and it was dusty.

"He'll bring it in." Whitey told him, real bossy like. Pete shook my hand and said he was glad he met me. He winked at Whitey, and after Pete gave Samson a drink of water out of an old hub cap, we were off again, going north on Dragster's Boulevard. We didn't stop in front of the Sheriff's office, but Whitey told me that Sheriff Chase didn't miss much. "He hangs out at Ron Dragston's Auto Repair when there isn't a burglary goin' on or something. He gets a cup of coffee from the back room, and they all smoke Lucky Strikes while they work on his heap."

We passed Drew's Tavern, and Whitey slowed up when we reached Spangler's Drug. "We gotta go in there real soon. There's a swell soda fountain. My mom takes me in there when she has a slow day." I reminded him that I had money for candy bars. In about two shakes, my pal was in the store and back out with two Baby Ruth bars.

At the corner of Dragster's and Willow Grove Road was an alley that wound diagonally back through the block where I lived. It was narrow, just wide enough for one car. It was lined with a sagging, wire fence and crooked posts. There were hollyhocks, trash cans, wheelbarrows and anything else that people wanted hidden from the street. At one place, we were accosted (from behind the fence, thankfully) by a chow dog. He came at us and slammed right into the fence, growling and snarling. "That's Victor. He belongs to the two guys that live there. He bit the paper boy a couple of years ago, and now they can't let him outside that fence, or they'll be in trouble. Samson was baring his teeth. His throat was doing that rumbling thing again. I had seen that before. The fur was up on his neck, head low and tail down. That *scary position*. He didn't move, but the chow yelped and squealed, running back to his dog house. "Samson causes that with bad dogs sometimes."

In short order, we were at the bottom of Spirit Hill Drive by the cemetery with the same name. "That's Old Man Woodard's place." The Woodard house sat up on the hill in the trees across the road from the cemetery. "He's got a big apple orchard, and you can probably see those trees when you look out your bedroom window."

"Do you know Mr. Woodard?"

"Yep. Hang on!" Whitey took off running like hell up the road toward the house, jerking the wagon and causing my legs to fly upward and me to flip, feet-over-head, out to the ground behind the wagon. I howled and called him a dumb turd, which was the worst thing I could think of at the time. My eyes were watering, and both elbows were skinned and bleeding. I had flipped upside down and hit my head on the back of the wagon.

"You coulda warned me you were gonna take off like that, you crummy twerp! Why do I always have to go through blood, sweat and tears with you? My mom is gonna kill both of us!"

I was blubbering, and my nose was all snotty. Samson was already on the job, licking the blood off my elbows and the snot off my face. I just let him. It was kind of soothing. My dad told me that a dog's mouth was antiseptic, anyway.

"Jeeze, I'm sorry, Thump." Whitey helped me back into the wagon and handed me my crutch, which had wound up in the weeds by the road. "You gonna be OK, buddy?"

Other than being shaken, I was OK. My face and elbows were clean and not even sore. I remember that bump on my head looked pretty bad the next day. Mom had had a fit about it.

Whitey took his time the rest of the way. Before we reached the front steps, a man in overalls and a plaid shirt stepped onto the porch. He had a coffee cup in his hand and carefully sat down on the swing, as if all his bones hurt or something. "Where you been, Little Guy? Haven't seen you in a while! Who's your pal? Want a soda pop?"

"I been around. This is Thump, uh, Warren. Yeah, we'd like a soda pop."

I gave him a wave from the wagon.

"You can call me Simon."

"Eunice! Whitey's got a new friend!" He yelled, and a woman with her hair braided up in a big knot came to the screened door. "This is Warren. Can you get these nice boys some root beers, Mama?" She told me how glad she was to meet me and how nice it was of Whitey to bring me out to the house with him. She disappeared and returned shortly with two cold bottles of root beer. Simon invited us to sit on the steps, and Eunice sat down on the swing next to the old man. I *thought* he was old, anyway. I was ten. Mr. Woodard asked me where I was from and how long I had been in Florence and a lot of other stuff. Whitey told him about the BEAMSHOOTER business. No questions were asked about my leg. It was as if they all knew about that ahead of time. I felt like I was almost *expected*.

"Eunice and I have the apple orchard out back, and that's how we met Mr. Whitey Swift, here! You're a lucky boy to know Whitey. He's a heck of a kid! When did you first come to our place, Little Guy?"

"My mom brought me out here to buy a sack of your apples. Remember? I was in third grade."

Mr. Woodard, I learned, always sold apples at a stand down on Spirit Hill Drive in front of the property. He told me how Whitey had spent one whole Saturday, helping sack the fruit in the fall. They sold pumpkins, along with potatoes and onions. They had about thirty peony bushes out back, and they sold them to people who were visiting Spirit Hill Cemetery on Memorial Day. Whitey had spent a lot of time there, taking in the love and attention of two people who had met him by accident.

"I stopped getting into trouble at school after I met the Woodard's." Whitey took a large swig of the root beer and belched loudly. "Woops. Sorry."

"Oh, think nothin' of it. You need something to wash that root beer down with." Mrs. Woodard disappeared into the house and came back with a plate of her homemade peanut butter cookies with the fork marks on the top. She threw one to Samson, who was asleep and having a dream. His legs were twitching, his chops were whiffling, and he was making little yipping noises. When Mrs. Woodard tossed the cookie in the air, Samson was airborne in less than a second, out of a dead sleep, with that cookie in his mouth.

I liked it out at the Woodard farm. I started to feel like I had known them forever, as we all sat crunching cookies and swigging root beer on the porch. It was peaceful. I wished they were my grandparents. Nobody can have too many grandparents.

"Well, whattya think, Trooper?" Mr. Woodard stood up, as if he was ready to go someplace. I liked the name, "Trooper." I think Mr. Woodard must have called a lot of kids that name. I think that's the reason I gave my grandson that nickname, many years later.

"Yeah, we better!" I think Whitey liked being called that.

"Better WHAT?" I was in the dark … again.

"You men go on. I have sheets to hang out in back while the sun is still shining!" Mrs. Woodard was a nice woman.

Whitey told me to get back in the wagon, because it was a little bit of a hike where we were headed. He *gently* started to pull me through the grass, around the house, and out to a big barn. Mr. Woodard was puffing and panting, so we traveled slowly. The wagon bumped over dirt and gravel and through weeds, as we went around the barn and out through the apple orchard.

"Criminey. Where are we GOIN'?" I was having a great time, but I was wondering what surprise Whitey had in store this time. So far, he was batting a thousand on unexpected adventures that had a way of leaving me with scars and bruises and making me have to explain something to my mother. I didn't want Mom to see my scraped elbows or the bump on my noggin. Samson was checking out the area, running through the tall weeds and bushes with his nose to the ground. He took a strained minute to hunker down and leave a dump. Yes, I do remember all the happenings of that summer, down to the littlest detail, just like it was yesterday.

"Look up there." Whitey pointed up the hill, as we came out of the apple trees. It was an old, OLD tree. Must have been there close to a hundred years, at least. It was all by itself at the top of the hill. The branches were twisted and bent, and much of the lower growth had broken off. There were leaves growing on what was left. It must have gone through many Nebraska tornadoes and blizzards. In the main fork, a weathered tree house sat. Some of the boards were crooked, and some were missing. I could see light coming through the slats. On the west side was a single window. Someone had hammered many nails into the tree trunk to make wooden ladder steps. Seven or eight steps to the top. The east side was accessible to enter, because there was a partial, half-wall. The other half must have had a canvas flap at one time. It had rotted off, but some scraps were still hanging there, blowing in the wind.

"Cool, huh?"

"Yeah. COOOOOL."

Old Man Woodard and Whitey looked at each other, as if there was something going on. Once again, I had the feeling I wasn't in on everything.

"I built that for my grandchildren, you know. The little ones always liked to come out here, especially Kenny. They spent a lot of time up there in the lookout. We called it Venus House. That was a long time ago. The grandchildren are all grown up now, but I keep poundin' a nail in, now and then, just to keep it from fallin' to pieces. It's my responsibility." Simon winked at Whitey.

I wanted to spring out of that stupid wagon and run like the wind to that tree and climb to the top of that ladder. If it was mine, I would have a CLUB, where only members could come, which wouldn't include that dumb Spider or Rat or that fat Weasel or Beverly and her giggling girl friends. We could take all our stuff up in the tree house and stay all night. It would be like camping up in the *air!* We could learn to smoke! We could have a password, like *ATOMIC,* and cut our fingers and press them together to mix our blood. Blood brothers! For a little while, I forgot my gimpy leg and the ugly brace and the stupid crutch.

"We gotta go now, Thump. Your mom said to be back for lunch." Whitey was obsessed about keeping in my mom's good graces. What a politician he was, and is.

"Right NOW?" I wasn't ready to leave yet. I was trying to figure out how a crippled boy could get up into that tree house. I thought, if I stayed there long enough, it would happen. If anybody could do it, Whitey could. I was mad at him, the little creep. He could do it if he wanted to. I remember glaring at him for the longest time, and this was the first time I noticed the scar by his hairline.

"We got big plans to make, Thump. You gotta be real patient. Let's go."

"What PLANS?" The wagon was moving, and Samson tried to jump in with me a couple of times. Whitey finally showed the dog some mercy and let Samson jump in the front, between my legs. It was a secure, warm feeling with my arms around his middle and my tummy against Samson's back. Mr. Woodard reached the porch after we did, and he was panting a bit.

"See you real soon, boys! I got some chores to do back at the tree house, but it'll be ready!"

"WHAT'LL be ready?" I just couldn't stand it.

"You'll find out when I tell you!" Whitey began to run, and we were back in my front yard in five minutes. He was so strong, it was scary.

"What's your mom fixin' for lunch?"

"I don't know. Probably cabbage and lima beans." I was feeling mean.

I didn't remember my mom asking him to lunch. I wasn't even thinking about that. I just couldn't wait to tell my mother about the tree house. Whitey stepped in front of me, stopping my attempt to stand up.

"You can't tell her about Venus House. There's a list of rules, Thump. I'm serious." My balloon was popped, and I thought I was going to cry, but I didn't. I was mad. Again. "You can tell her about everything *else*, just for now, but not the tree house. OK?"

"You're a creep, you know that?" We started for my porch, when Mom met us at the door.

"You'll stay for lunch, won't you Duane?"

He had my mom in the palm of his hand. It wasn't long before we were at the kitchen table, eating homemade potato soup and crackers. I was jabbering on and on about my trip around town, but not about Venus House. Samson was sprinkling several square feet of the linoleum as he slurped from a bowl of water.

Beverly wasn't home, as usual. Her meals didn't seem to coincide with mine in those days. She was sixteen, you remember.

Mom had gone into the bathroom, so Whitey took advantage of the privacy. "I'll lay out the plan after lunch. Can I stay a while, or is your mom gonna make you take a NAP?" Whitey used that whiney sound when he said the word NAP. I wanted to punch him in the nose, but I couldn't, because he probably wouldn't tell me the *plan*. He had me over a barrel.

Mom came back to the kitchen as we finished lunch. Whitey beamed at Mom and thanked her for the soup. "It's all right if you want to stay, Duane. I just think Warren should take it easy up in his room for a little while. He can tell me about his skinned elbows and that bump on his head later." Mom glared at me and didn't press me for quick answers. Whitey had done it again.

THE WOODARD FARM

12

GETAWAY

I've consumed three or four cups of leaded coffee and hit the bathroom several times by two AM, when I hear an engine out front. If a person can tiptoe in a truck, that's what Whitey is doing as he creeps into my driveway, barely touching the gas pedal and traveling about .01 miles per hour. The headlights are off, probably snuffed a block away from my house. It seems stupid for Whitey to have to travel out of the way to pick me up and then back-track to his own neighborhood where the action is to take place. Woodard's house is less than ten minutes from Whitey's place, but he's the guy with the truck, and I need to load my gear in the back.

I meet him at the side door of the kitchen. We're quietly putting my tools in the truck bed, which has a blanket in the bottom for noise control. We're being careful not to cause Wilber and Rose next door to wake up and call the police. Sign language and whispers are the communication as we load up. There simply isn't any reason for two old guys to be leaving their warm beds at this hour, and we can't afford any trouble. We have no margin for error and no excuses for being out in the wee hours if we have a problem … and if the police get involved.

We chunk the doors shut, and Whitey leaves the headlights off until we are a block away from my place. He's wired tighter than a squirrel in heat and chewing gum so fast, I worry he might bite his tongue and scream, and it would all be over. He's wearing his black stocking cap, like any other robber would. Whitey grabs a Corona from a six pack on the floor by my feet. He's holding the lip of the cap on the edge of the ash tray and swiping it downward, which pops the cap right off. He takes a long swig and sticks the thing between his legs. It is quite a vision.

"Want one?" His eyes look weird in the lights of the dashboard, especially with his half-inch-thick glasses. He never wears his specs, unless there is a crisis. He once told me that he hated wearing the ugly things, but he admitted that his pink eyes didn't see too well. With his stocking cap over his head and the over-sized lenses, Whitey resembles some kind of bug. I'm keeping this to myself.

"Think I'll hold off on the brew till we get through the dicey stuff." How much work can a guy get done when he's whizzing in the weeds every five minutes?

"I'm thinkin' we should circle clear around Florence and hit the Woodard place from the north. I don't want anybody spottin' my vehicle. It was ELEVEN before that Petty woman left! So much for a little rest! Them two women just HAD to get out the cookie mix and make 'em for us. They smelled awful good, I had to admit. I let the women each have one, and brought all the rest for you and me, Buddy. Have one." Whitey grabs a plastic zipper bag from the top of his cluttered dashboard.

My TV dinner isn't sticking to my ribs, so I help myself to about three of the chocolate chip wonders and decide that a beer would taste pretty good with them, after all. My own dad used to say that beer and chocolate were a good combination. He was right. We're staying off the main drags, as we make our way back north toward Florence. Somehow, Whitey now has us on a county road north of town. We're headed back south again, and to my surprise, we find ourselves on Willow Grove Road which runs along the north edge of the Woodard property.

"Help me watch for the turn-in, Thump." I wouldn't have known about any turn-in, but I watch along the side of the gravel road, as Whitey's tires crunch over the uneven dirt and rocks. I see two bright eyes disappear into the weeds. Probably a raccoon or a possum. There's a break in the vegetation and a post with a small, white wooden sign on it. PRIVATE PROPERTY.

"Ain't PRIVATE to me. Old Man Woodard told me we were always welcome here. Just because he's dead, and we're comin' in the back way, doesn't negate that invitation. By the way, Pal, I just found out that Miss Petty Cash is a private investigator." Whitey pops another whole cookie in his mouth and washes it down with the second half of that Corona. "No wonder she read all the crap we wrote on those placemats."

"You gotta be shittin' me." I almost choke on my beer.

"I don't really believe it either. If you ask me, I think she just said that to turn me on."

I'm wondering if Whitey had a beer or two before he picked me up. We hang a right and wheel straight down into a ditch. Whitey guns the engine, sending dirt and rocks flying out behind us. I hit my head on the ceiling of the cab, as we fly out of the gully and into the rough ground around the orchard. As usual, I figure I'll probably go home with an injury. It's normal on an outing with Whitey. Always been that way, so why should it change now, just because we're old farts?

We head west, circling the perimeter of the orchard. I can see the tree in the headlights and the remaining boards of the tree house. Much of the wood is now lying on the ground. Over the years, the nails have fallen from the trunk, and some of the wood slats have just plain given up.

"Makes a person feel kinda sad, doesn't it?"

"Yep, it does. Listen. Ya ever hear the sound, when there ain't nothin'?" Whitey whispers.

"Yeah … back in '49. Right here, one night. The stars were unbelievable, just like they are now. Don't get to see much of the sky where I live. Too many trees and light pollution. Old Man Woodard showed us the big dipper and how it pointed to Polaris. Said we never would be lost with that information in our heads. Remember? Can't see the dipper this late, but Polaris is there. It's the only star that doesn't move west during the night, he told us. And then there's Venus."

"Yep. Venus. Goddess of love and beauty. Brightest star. Did ya know that all her surface features are named after females? Can't see her right now. Too late. She's gone till tomorrow when she shows up again in the west after the sun's gone down. Sometimes, they call her Lucifer when she's in the east in the morning. Then there'll be a stretch when you'll only see her in the west, after sundown. A guy wouldn't last long on Venus, Buddy. High winds, and her surface temperature is hot enough to melt lead, but she's our sister planet and ya gotta love her." Whitey is in a mellow mood now, which is unusual for him. He pops another beer, and I'm beginning to get concerned about his equilibrium and judgment, in light of the fact that we are setting out to climb a damn tree.

We sit in the truck with our heads tilted out the open windows, gazing at the sky, like we did when we were ten and lying on the ground, looking up at the clouds that summer.

"'Nuf of this. We gotta move along before we run out of DARK, Buddy. I think we can leave the truck right here. No sense in trying to hide it. Nobody followed us, and there ain't a house that I can see from here. Let's get to it."

13

THE LOWDOWN

"Your mom makes good soup." Whitey's comments had a way of reminding me that I had it pretty darn good, in spite of my health problems. We trudged up the stairs to my room. I was tired after my exciting trip to the Woodard place. We both flopped onto my bed, along with Samson, of course. I asked Whitey if his mother was a good cook. He told me she was, but that his Grandma Mac did most of the meals, since his mother had to work most of the time.

"I hate it when Grandma makes kraut and weenies or bean soup. She doesn't cook like my mom. I always tell her I would rather have peanut butter, but Mom makes me be nice and tells me to eat the stuff anyway. But Saturday nights are the BEST, because Mom makes macaroni and cheese for me … every single Saturday night."

"I like macaroni, too. I'll bet your mom makes it real good."

"Maybe you could come to my house for supper some Saturday night. Maybe THIS Saturday! That's *tomorrow* … and maybe stay all night!" Whitey smiled real big. He was a special, good guy who didn't know it. I even wondered if I might have been his first or only best friend ever.

"That would be cool!" I had slight reservations about his grandma and that snoring thing, however. I yelled down the steps at Mom and asked her could I please stay all night at Whitey's house tomorrow. I even added the "pleases", just like Beverly always did. I wasn't surprised that Mom wouldn't give me an immediate answer.

"Duane, have your mother call me when she gets home from work today, and we'll see." Mom said from the bottom of the steps. My mom was being true to herself, but I had the feeling the answer would be a "yes" with all of the added cautions and rules. It would depend on how the telephone conversation went between our two moms.

Whitey kicked into his aggressive, high gear. "Mrs. Hearst, can I call my mom at her shop and ask her right now?" Then, Whitey whispered to me. "If she's real busy, she might say yes, just to make me quit buggin' her."

"Well, I suppose so. I hope your mother won't be cross with me for letting you call her at work, Duane."

"She won't!" Whitey punched me in the arm like he had won something big. "Cross your fingers, Thump … be right back!" I sat on my bed along with Samson. I was rubbing my arm where I had taken Whitey's punch. I could hear my friend on the phone down in the hallway, and I knew my mom would be standing right next to him. "Kenwood 0822." He told the operator. Pretty soon, I heard him say "Hi, Mom." I couldn't hear much, but it was a sales pitch, for sure Mom told Whitey to let her have the phone, which didn't surprise me. I heard little bits of the conversation. I knew Mom would make sure that Whitey's Mom sounded at least sane.

"Hello, Norma. I'm Dorothy." In a minute or two, Whitey raced up the steps and took a flying leap onto my bed, causing Samson and me to bounce.

"My job is done. Sure hope the rest of it flies."

It wasn't long before Mom trudged up the steps. "I guess it'll be OK, Warren, unless your father objects. But I don't think he will. I know it's not far away, but we have to talk about the rules. You can stay until three, Duane, and then Warren needs take a rest before we have supper. Does your grandmother know where you are?"

"Yeah, I told her I would be here all day. She doesn't plan on me for lunch, unless she sees me." The rules at the Swift residence were much looser than they ever were at my house.

We were flat on or backs on my bed, having a contest to see who could blow the hardest and make my hanging airplanes move the most, when Whitey turned to his side and faced me. "Okay, Buddy. Here's the dope." I wondered what he was talking about, because, as far as I knew, the plans were being made for me to stay all night at his house. Was there something extra that I didn't catch? Then, I remembered that mysterious *plan* Whitey mentioned at Woodard's house.

"Okay, tell me the *dope*, already!"

Whitey was scratching Samson's belly and staring at me over the large mound of dog. "You gotta get yourself ready for a big session of explainin' to your folks when you get home on Sunday morning."

I started to protest that I just couldn't come home again with another injury, because my mom would probably keep me from being anywhere near Duane Swift forever. Whitey interrupted me, whispering intensely and freezing me with his pink eyes. "I ain't kiddin' you, Thump. We're gonna have to be a TEAM! I know we are already a team, but tomorrow we *really* have to be!" Then Whitey asked me if I ever prayed. I told him we said a prayer at the table sometimes, especially at Thanksgiving. "Well, you better do it tonight when you go to bed, because we gotta have good weather tomorrow night with NO CLOUDS! Got it?"

I was in the dark and getting mad again, because I was without a clue.

"Criminey! Would you mind tellin' me what the heck is going on?" I know my neck cords were standing out, as they always were when I was frustrated and wanting to choke somebody.

I realize, dear reader, that you must be confused as to why I remember these conversations. Trust me. It'll come clear in good time.

"Do you have guts, Buddy? Are you brave?" Whitey propped his chin on Samson's rib cage. His eyes were in that persuasive mode again. "I wanna know if you are a man or a mouse!"

"Yeah, I'm brave. I'm still here after all the junk you put me through all the time, ain't I? I can take anything you can dish out, you little creep!"

"Atta boy. So, here's the deal. Your mom is coming to my house in the morning. I know that your mom is gonna make sure she likes mine before she'll let you stay all night with me. I heard this end of the conversation while I was downstairs with her. You're comin' for supper; because I want you to have my mom's macaroni and cheese, and your dad is gonna walk with you when you come. He might bring you in my wagon if you want to ride, but something tells me you won't, because *you got guts and you're brave and you can take anything I can dish out!*"

Whitey can get real bossy. I want to shove him off the bed, right along with his dog.

Whitey had a few more instructions for me before he left. "Tell your mom that we might go out and catch lightening bugs, and tell her I'm gonna show you my fort and soldiers out by the shed. After that, we're gonna listen to the radio in my room and eat more stuff. That ought to satisfy her that we have plans to have fun and not get into any trouble. I'll tell you the rest tomorrow. That's all you need to know, for now." I found out later that there was a lot more to it than that. The little creep.

◆   ◆   ◆

"When are we going over to meet Mrs. Swift, Mom?" We were all at the breakfast table, which was the usual on Saturday mornings when Dad was home. Even Beverly was there, because it was a rule on the week ends. Dad was browsing the paper, and Beverly was looking at TIME MAGAZINE, which happened to have a picture of Princess Margaret on the cover. I didn't know who she was at the time, but she must have been important. We had had pancakes with bacon, and the kitchen smelled so good. Now, I have to go to the Pancake House for that aroma.

"I'm going over to see Mrs. Swift at ten, Warren, but I'm going by myself. I want a chance to visit without you and Whitey trying to lead the conversation." Dad put his paper down.

"Hey, Rastus, I need to get the car gassed up. Want to go?" Of course, I wanted to go. Being with Dad and the guys at the gas station was always a good time for me. Ron, the owner, always gave me a candy bar or a bottle of Coke. I know my dad figured this was a way of keeping me busy. I was anxious to go to Whitey's house. Mom smiled at Dad, and he winked at her. I saw.

Beverly always had plans in the coffer. "Can I go over to Virginia's after I clean my room? We're going to show Patty how to stuff her bra. She's always complaining about her body, she's so straight up and down."

"Beverly, you can go, but you need to be home by lunch time. By the way, you tell Patty that she'll be thankful someday that she is so slim. Besides, when she's older she'll find out about falsies if she is that desperate. Just be thankful that all three of you are lovely girls!" Another Mom lecture. "The bathroom needs a lick and a promise before you go."

This was a typical Saturday morning. Mom was doing up the dishes, Beverly hurried off to get her chores done, and Dad and I headed for the gas station. I wondered what Mom and Mrs. Swift would say to each other, and I wondered what Grandma Mac would be like, too. I guessed that the day would pass, and I would finally know.

◆　　　◆　　　◆

It was about four o'clock, and I was in the tub. I was starting to feel sorry for myself again. This happened from time to time. My dumb crutch was leaning on the door, and the crummy brace was lying on the toilet seat. How simple things would be if those clunky devices weren't part of my life. It wasn't fair. The warm water felt good with the freedom of no brace on my leg. The bathroom was always that place where you could cry if you wanted to, and nobody would know, because your face would already be wet. I was feeling kind of drowsy in the warm bath, when I heard Mom and Dad talking in the kitchen …

"It was an enlightening experience over at Duane's house, Bernie. It's no wonder that Whitey spends so much time here. That child need some male role models, I can tell you that!"

Then, I heard Mom say that she had a few minutes to talk to Grandma Mac alone, while they waited for Norma (Whitey's mom) to get back from the store with some cinnamon roles to go with coffee. "I finally got up the nerve to inquire about Duane's father … well, did *that* ever open up a can of worms! By the way,

Bernie, Grandma Mac isn't that old! She's probably in her late fifties. The name "Mac" comes from her husband's last name, which was MacEwen. Scottish, I guess. But, getting back to Duane's father … an *animal!* Norma brought Duane from South Dakota with her when the boy was about seven. Packed up some bare essentials and took off on a bus at midnight, while Duane's father was at work on a night shift. Grandma Mac had tears in her eyes when she told me the sorry state her daughter and grandson were in when they arrived. Norma was covered with bruises and had a broken nose. Duane had a bandage on his forehead and a broken ear drum. They had been living in a God-forsaken, dumpy trailer court with no other family around for support. She said that Duane's father used to call him "Little Spook". Anyway, Grandma Mac gave Norma the money to open up her own shop over there on Thirtieth Street, and they've been with her ever since. The straw that broke the camel's back happened when Duane's father dragged the boy into the woods behind the trailer court in a rage. He had a gun. He told Norma to stay inside or he would put a bullet in her. Then, he took poor little Duane into the woods and shot his dog, right in front of him!"

I heard my mom kind of whimper. "That's about the time Norma showed up with the rolls. She was really nice, Bernie. I liked her. She's trying real hard at being a good mother."

"I can't even understand jerks like her husband. You'll keep ME in line, won't you?"

"Don't worry, Buster." I heard Mom blow her nose. I know they must have been hugging each other, because it got quiet. My mom was upset. I was being real quiet and not splashing the water, because I wanted to hear what my folks were saying. I started to worry that Mom might not let me go over there. That wouldn't be fair. It wasn't Whitey's fault that his dad was a monster.

It wasn't until later that I found out why no one has seen the Monster since then.

14

YOU CAN'T WIN 'EM ALL

"Y'see that?" Whitey says to me just as we're getting ready to get out of the truck. I'm not seeing, because I'm busy taking a pee from all the coffee and the beer. He's pointing up at the tree house, which is now glowing with a real faint, blue haze around it. I hadn't noticed that when we first got here. I do remember that particular phenomenon from way back then, however. I'm the kid that hasn't forgotten anything about this special hideout. It's as if the thing *knows* us, and I'm not foolin!

I make the suggestion that Whitey back the truck right up to the tree to save us hauling everything so far, which he does, after about five tries and several loops and circles. I yell, "Whoa!" and the truck stops only an inch from the tree trunk.

My partner in crime slides out of the cab and sets his Corona on the roof. "Let's put the tools out on the ground so we won't bury any of 'em while we're doin' the demo work." Whitey seems to be thinking fairly straight, so that's what we do. "You get up into the truck bed and take the stuff when I hand it down, that sound OK?"

I don't know whether it sounds OK. I'm concerned about safety and *height* and *beer,* which doesn't sound like a good combination. But, up he goes, wearing his leather tool belt full of anything he might need. He's got a flashlight in his mouth. I can't begin to describe that man with the thick glasses, those pink eyes, that black stocking cap and a headlight in his mouth. I remind him to be careful. Whitey hammers some new nails into the crude steps that are barely hanging on the trunk before he puts any weight on them. Whitey ran the Thirtieth Street Hardware Store for many years and did carpenter work on the side, so I figure he's the man for this demo work.

"It's still viable, Buddy. Feel this." Whitey hands down the first of the roof slats. It's warm to the touch, in spite of the cold weather. Makes my hand tingle, even through my work gloves. Oh yeah, I remember this, all right. There's a strange vapor around each piece, much like what rises from dry ice.

Within a short time, I'm taking wood slats from him at a pretty darn good pace and tossing them into the back of the truck. All the time, I'm searching the area for possible intruders as he works industriously, prying out rusty nails, pounding on wood slats to get them loose, and swearing now and then. Often, in fact. He is now on the last wall with only a few pieces to hand down before we tackle the floor, which happens to be a couple of large pieces of some kind of wood with swirly grain.

"Get a gander at THIS, Buddy!" Whitey climbs down with a slat of the wood that is wider than the rest. "We don't want to lose this one. I think it's the record! Lookit here!" He puts the beam of the flashlight on it for me to inspect. "Old man Woodard musta done this after you and I were there when we were ten! There are five names on it, carved right into it with dates, including *ours*! I feel like I'm lookin' at somethin' *sacred!*"

SIMON WOODARD JUNE 1924
WILMA WOODARD JUNE 1926
KENNY WOODARD JUNE 1944
DUANE SWIFT JUNE 1946
WARREN HEARST JUNE 1949

"We can talk about the names sometime later, Buddy. It's goin' on three thirty, and we gotta finish up."

While my pal and I were in grade school, we continued to visit the tree house, but we got older, strangely. I had gotten taken up with my life, just like Whitey did, and keeping vigil on our old hideout wasn't part of it. I don't know when Mr. Woodard put my name on the ledger.

I decide to slip the "record board" up in the cab, as Whitey is prying the floor away with a crow bar.

"Here's the first half of the floor, Buddy." Whitey wrestles with the cumbersome piece of wood and lets one end of it drop down into my palms. "Back up!"

He's sounding a little less patient than he was when we started this project. I do as he tells me, and his end of the floor slaps into the truck bed … my end of the slab bangs into both of my shins on its way down. Here is my first injury for this adventure with Whitey, and there is now blood seeping through both legs of my pants. I'm wrong about that … I did bump my head in the cab of the truck on the way in when we drove up out of that ditch.

"Judas!"

"You okay, Thump?" I've heard that question before from my friend, and I tell him I think I'll live. After a few more cuss words and grunts and hammer whacks, Whitey is lowering himself down to the top ladder step. "The other half of the floor is loose now. All I have to do is pull it over and let it follow me down the lad …"

Whitey comes crashing down into the truck bed as the second ladder step from the top gives way. The corner of the floor slab slashes me on the forehead, and I realize that I have a nasty gash when something wet runs into my left eye. It is quiet for a minute or two, except for some groaning on Whitey's part and some heavy breathing on mine. There is warmth radiating from each piece of wood, including the one large slab that partially covers Whitey like a blanket. Our breath is coming out in puffs in the night air, and it is colder than a well digger's you-know-what.

"Shit." Whitey is on his back, under the piece of flooring.

"Shit, right back to *you*." I'm wiping my eye on my sleeve. I have fallen on my keester, trying to catch Whitey, so here I sit.

Whitey and I don't move. We seem to be assessing the damage before we do anything dumb and hurt ourselves even more than we already have.

"Can you shove this piece of wood off me? I think I broke my ankle, and it looks to me like you're gonna have to drive home, Buddy."

"I'm taking you to emergency."

"It could be a little awkward. What's the story gonna be? It's the middle of the night. Old farts should be in bed by now."

"You were home alone; your wife was out of town. You fell down the steps sleep walking in the middle of the night, and you crawled to the telephone in the kitchen to call me. End of story."

"It smells. How are you gonna explain the blood on *your* pants and the gash on *your* noggin?"

"I got in a fight on my way to pick you up?"

It's obvious that Whitey isn't in the mood for fun and games, so I'm thinking real fast. "Alternate plan, my friend. I drive you home now and help you take a shower. While I'm cleaning up, Connie can help you throw some fresh clothes on after she gets through yelling at us, and I'll borrow a clean pair of pants and a jacket that isn't bloody from you and put a bandage over my gash. If Connie isn't too mad at us, she can fix us some breakfast, and that'll kill some time. We go to emergency, and you tell them you fell down the steps early this morning … tripped over the dog, maybe. Let 'em think you were alone in the house, so you had to call me. If they ask me about my head problem, I tell them I whacked it while I was working under the car yesterday. By the time we actually get there, it'll be daylight. Things won't look quite as suspicious. If they ask any embarrassing questions, we wing it."

Whitey just stares at me for several seconds with those spooky, pink pupils of his.

"Well, I guess it's better than trying to explain why we were out at two in the morning, dressed like cat burglars and stealing a tree house, one board at a time, off of somebody else's damn private property."

I'm now unlocking all my joints into a standing position, so that I can climb out of the truck bed and put the tailgate down. Whitey is surprisingly helpful in this effort. He has removed his tool belt and manages to scoot to the back and drop down to the ground on his good leg. I tell him to put his arm on my shoulder. We're doing the SHOTTISH together as Whitey hops on one foot to the passenger door. With him safely in, I'm putting the tailgate back up, removing the CORONA from the cab roof and dumping its contents on the ground. We have harvested most of the wood, which is now rattling around and glowing, phosphorescent blue, in the truck bed, as we're bouncing back to the main road. I'm nervous about the faint haze that's hovering over the pile of wood that once was our hideout, and I'm hoping we can get home without somebody noticing that. I'm just too tired to try digging the tarp out from under everything to hide the load.

"I'm in real bad pain, Buddy. I don't think I'll be walking on this ankle for awhile." Whitey acts drowsy. Probably a bit of shock, along with several beers, I'm guessing.

"Yeah, Pal. I can relate to that leg problem."

15

LIFE BEGINS AT TEN

The bath felt real good. I used to get all stiff and sore sometimes from not moving around much, and I was having one of those days. I was excited about going to Whitey's house, but at the same time I was kind of low. I kept thinking of all the fun I could have with this new friend, if only I could just get up out of that tub and not have to put on the stupid brace. If only I could throw the crutch out the window and never see it again. If only I could run and jump and climb trees and play shortstop and ride my bike. If only.

I was letting myself get into a bad funk, when Dad opened the bathroom door and peeked in. "Can I help you, Rastus?" Dad always seemed to know when I needed a budge. A ten-year-old kid doesn't like to feel helpless, and I certainly wasn't. But I let my dad pull me up and lift me out of the tub this time. Sometimes, a guy just gives it up a little. He wrapped the towel around me and offered to help me dress and put the brace on my leg.

"I can do it, Dad."

"I know. You're a tough kid." He still helped me. It's times like this that tell you you're a lucky stiff to have a good dad and mom and even a good sis who is nice to you most of the time.

I could smell fresh baked cookies as Dad and I came into the kitchen where Mom was cutting up onions.

"Dad and I are having liver and onions and brussel sprouts while you're at Whitey's." I thought that was good planning on her part and thanked her. "Your sister is having supper at Patty's house with Virginia. They're having a slumber party." I was thinking that my parents were going to be awful bored with every-body gone for the whole night.

Mom had put my pajamas, tooth brush, clean underwear and my comb into a pillow case. "Anything else you want to take over there?" I told her I didn't think so, and I told her all the plans for the evening. Mom was slipping my favorite chocolate chip cookies into a used bread wrapper. She saved all those bread bags with the polka dots on them to put Dad's lunches in. There was a whole drawer full of them. "Dad's going to carry your stuff and walk over there with you. It's almost five, so you can go now. Give me a kiss. You smell so nice and clean!"

I gave her a kiss, even though I was only going across the street and down two houses and only staying overnight. Whitey, his mom and Samson were watching us from the porch steps before we even got there. "This is my dog. His name is Samson, and he's real friendly. And this is my mom." I don't think Whitey was used to introducing people. I noticed that the dog came first.

"Hello, Mr. Hearst. I'm Norma Swift. We're so glad Warren could spend the night. We've heard so much about him from Whitey, and I think the boys will have a wonderful time! I made my famous macaroni and cheese. It's my son's favorite." Dad gave her the cookies, and she seemed a little surprised and nervous talking to him. Thinking back on the conversation that I overheard between Mom and Dad in the kitchen about Whitey's father, I realized that Mrs. Swift might have been cautious talking to any man. "Cookies! How nice! Thank you."

Knowing what I know now, I figure that Whitey's Mom wouldn't have expected to see any *man* carrying a plate of cookies to anyone. That was a woman's work.

"Warren's been looking forward to this all day." Dad ruffled my hair and told me to behave myself and have a good time. I felt kind of bad when he went home, because he was going to have to eat liver and onions all alone with Mom.

Whitey carried my stuff and took me down the hall to the back of the house where his room was. I could hear Mrs. Hearst talking in the kitchen. I guessed that it must have been his Grandma Mac out there with her. Whitey's room wasn't very big. It had a twin bed, and there were some cushions from the sofa on the floor next to it. "I'm sleeping on the floor next to you. You're *company*, so you get the bed." Whitey showed me his stuff, much of which was under his bed and in the bottom of his little closet. He had a lot of cool soldiers and tanks and cars, and he told me he would show me where he made a battlefield in the dirt out back by the shed … just as he planned.

"Soup's on!" We heard from the kitchen. I got to meet Grandma Mac, who was putting some pineapple and cottage cheese and lettuce salads by our plates. I never had had that kind of salad, but it looked good. There was a huge pan of gooey, yellow macaroni and cheese sitting on a pad in the center of the table. "Sit! Don't be bashful, Warren." There was a glass of milk by my plate. "Say Grace, Whitey."

"Thank You for this good food, God … and for my friend. Amen."

It was a quick prayer, and Mrs. Swift shoveled a pile of the macaroni on each of our plates. It smelled real good, and to this day I love macaroni and cheese, except when it comes in a cardboard box with film over the top.

Whitey was strung tight all through supper. He acted like he had an appointment in an hour, but it didn't stop him from eating a big plate full with second helpings. Grandma Mac asked me if I was a member of the CLEAN PLATE CLUB. I said no, but I usually cleaned my plate anyway. "We must remember that there are starving children over in Europe." I didn't quite get what that had to do with my own plate, but I nodded "yes" and shoveled it in.

"Can I show Thump my battlefield out back before it gets dark?" His mom said he could.

"You two can have some of these wonderful cookies when you come in and listen to EDGAR BERGEN and CHARLIE McCARTHY in your room."

"Can we be excused?"

"What do you say to your mother, Whitey?" Grandma Mac said.

"Thanks for the supper, Ma."

"Yeah. Thanks." I added as Whitey jumped up from the table, and Samson wiggled out from between the table legs. Grandma Mac was nice and not even scary looking.

It was about six thirty when Samson crowded ahead of us on the way out the back door to see the battlefield. Some soldiers were down in little trenches that Whitey had dug. Others were positioned around in the hills waiting for the enemy. There was one very large crater that must have been dug by the dog.

"Cool, huh?"

"Yeah, Coooool. I could bring my soldiers over, and we could have a battle!"

Then, Whitey started whispering for me to come sit on a wooden bench by the shed. "We don't have much time, but here's the plan."

"WHAT plan?" I had been waiting for what seemed like forever to hear the *plan*.

"I gotta talk fast, 'cause we got lots to do. We're gonna look at this battlefield for about five minutes, and then we go in for cookies and CHARLIE McCAR-THY in my room. We goof around with my cars and look at comics. When it starts to get dark we'll watch lightening bugs for a few minutes. Then we get under the covers about eight thirty and listen to the radio and talk. I think Duffy's Tavern is on. Don't take off your clothes or nuthin'. Mom will probably look in and tell us not to stay awake too late, but she'll kind of leave us alone after that, I think. I'm gonna tell her that you're used to being asleep before nine since you were real sick, and I'll shut the bedroom door. We put a bunch of junk under the sheets to make it look like we're in bed asleep. Then we go out my window. If she finds out we're gone, we'll probably be in real hot water, but it'll be worth it. Trust me. Don't ask any questions now. Just play along with me like you always do. Let's go in and have the cookies."

Whitey's eyes were darting from side to side and up and down. They were glassy and glowing. I recognized that look, believe me.

"Criminey. You're out of your cotton-pickin' mind!" Whitey said there wasn't any time to argue, so I shut my trap and clumped along behind him to his bedroom. I had a bad feeling about climbing out Whitey's bedroom window. I just knew I would probably break my good leg.

◆   ◆   ◆

We sat on the sofa cushions that were on the floor and leaned on the bed while we ate cookies and drank the second glass of milk of the evening. CHARLIE McCARTHY was giving EDGAR BERGEN a hard time on the radio. We talked baseball. It was half-hearted on my part, since I couldn't play on a team anymore; but I told Whitey about some cool plays that I had pulled off when I was short-stop. We talked about how we would be able to watch a game on a new thing called *television*. My dad was planning on getting one, and when I told Whitey this, his pink eyes got real big. I told him he would have to come over and watch with me. I didn't need to ask him. He was always there anyway, the crazy little twerp.

The cookies and milk were rumbling around in our stomachs when we crawled under the sheets, me in the bed and Whitey on the floor cushions. It wasn't eight thirty yet when Mrs. Swift opened the door quietly. "You two OK?"

"Fine, Ma. We're just talkin'."

"See you in the morning. We're having pancakes!" The door clicked shut.

For the first time on that night it was quiet. The room was getting darker, but here was still a hint of pink in the western sky. There was a breeze blowing through the open window. It smelled fresh, like flowers, and there was a cardinal going *chip-chip* somewhere. First one up in the morning, last one to bed at the end of the day. I didn't notice those kinds of things when I was ten, but I do now. Old age is more aware of Mother Nature.

"You're lucky." Whitey looked up at me from the floor.

"What do you mean?"

"Your mom and dad. They're cool."

"Your mom and grandma are cool."

"Yeah."

It was so quiet. Then I took a big risk. "Where *is* your dad?"

"Gone."

"Just ... GONE?"

"Forever."

"Not ever coming back?"

"Dead."

"How?"

"You promise not to say anything to anybody, ever? Not even to your mom and dad or my mom or Grandma Mac?"

I promised, and I meant it.

Whitey told me the story about how his father was real mean and angry all the time. How his mother was afraid of his dad. How his dad had beaten her. How his dad had shot his little dog. How he hated having a monster for a father.

"Why did he shoot your dog?"

"I kicked my dad in the balls after he hurt my mom. He was a monster."

"Where did you live then?"

"South Dakota in a crummy trailer."

"How did the monst ... your dad die?"

"It was after Mom and I moved here to live with Grandma Mac, and I met Mr. Woodard and got that gift. The one I used on the school playground."

"What's that got to do with Old Man Woodard?"

"You'll know soon enough."

It was like pulling teeth to get anything out of Whitey, but I kept it up as long as he would talk.

"How *did* your dad die?" This was the big question, and Whitey didn't answer right away, but in a few seconds he started talking.

"Me and Mom and Grandma Mac went to get some ice cream one night after supper. We like to do that when the weather is nice and warm. Later, I went to bed, but Mom and Grandma were playing rummy in the front room and listening to AMOS 'n ANDY. I heard a tap on my bedroom window, and when I looked up, there was the monster all the way from South Dakota. He said for me to crawl out the window and told me I was gonna go live with him. He told me to keep my mouth shut, or he would break in the front door and slice my mom into pieces. I was real scared, and I promised I wouldn't make a noise. He reached up and grabbed my arms and swung me to the ground. Then he grabbed me by my hair and started walking away from the house. I kept stumbling. He was walking too fast. There was a car parked at the curb. He pushed me into the seat and shut the door as quiet as he could. I knew I had to do something real quick before he got me too far away. I just sat there while he walked around the car and got in. I turned sideways and started to stare at him as he was starting the engine. I stared *real* hard, and my dad looked real confused at me when I finally started talking to him.

"You have a real bad tummy ache, don't ya, Dad?" That's when he kind of grabbed his middle and squeezed his eyes shut. "You have to get out of the car to feel better." That monster got out of the car real quick, just as he threw up all over. I'm good at causing the throwing up stuff. "You gotta walk and walk, and you'll feel better. Walk down to River Road and get on the railroad tracks and follow them, and you'll be well again, Dad" I ordered him to do that, and he had to, because that's what I could *make* him do. It was kind of like what I did to those goons on the school playground. Anyway, he was lookin' at me like I was out of my mind, and he couldn't figure out why he was doin' exactly what I told him to do. It was the *gift*, Thump! He kept lookin' at my eyes. He was REAL scared, because he didn't have any control over me, and he couldn't make himself stop walking. "Walk faster, you bastard! To the tracks. Do you hear the train whistle? Walk to the tracks. Get on the tracks and walk toward the train, and you won't suffer anymore. No more tummy ache for Mr. Monster!" He kept walking right down the tracks toward the train. I was trotting along beside him, but not too close. I wasn't on the *tracks* like he was! The train was coming fast, and the whistle was blowing and blowing, because the engineer could see him. I couldn't even hear any bump when the train hit him because of the noise of the locomotive. My dad was mowed down and chewed up under the wheels, like when you run over a worm with your bike. I walked back home. It was probably about six blocks from my house. I crawled back in through my bedroom window and jumped into bed and didn't ever say anything to Ma or Grandma. I stayed under the sheet when the sirens came down the street, and I kept quiet. It took me a long time to quit shaking. Mom and Grandma Mac never knew nothin'. In a couple of days the cops towed the car away, and I was glad. Everybody was complaining about it and wondering where it came from. I just wanted it to go away. I didn't want to look at it all the time. It had Iowa license plates, and it was probably stolen. I don't think anybody ever found out who was splattered all over. I used to like the sound of train whistles, but not any more. Not after that."

◆   ◆   ◆

What does a guy say when he hears a story like that? Whitey was quiet for quite a while, and I just laid there not saying anything right along with him. Even in the dark, I could tell he was trying not to cry. Samson's head was snuggled up under Whitey's chin. Dogs worry when their masters are suffering. Dogs know.

"It's time." Whitey whispered, and the two of us tried not to make any noise while we stuffed a lot of his junk under our covers to make it look like there was a kid sleeping there. "My bike is by the house near the window."

"Your BIKE?"

"Shhhh!"

I was again in the dark and not knowing what was going to happen. It sounded to me like we were headed for big trouble with our parents. I never would have thought about going somewhere on a bike after I had already gone to bed … behind my parents' back!

The window was open, but Whitey carefully pushed it open wider for our exit. "I'll go out first, then you, Thump. I'll bend over and you can back out feet first and step on my back."

I was all ready to protest on the grounds that I probably would break my *good* leg, but my pal was already out and on the grass below. "Ready, Thump?"

I knew I had to move, and I was worried that Mrs. Swift would come checking on us and open the bedroom door just as I was half way out the window. That would be the end of whatever Whitey was planning. I grabbed my bad leg and heaved it up over the sill. I was straddling the darn thing. I engineered my good leg out and rolled over on my stomach. My feet were hanging outside, and my arms and head were inside. Samson was still in the room licking me on the mouth. "Let yourself drop down on my back! Hurry!"

"Criminey!" My brace hit the side of the house. Mrs. Swift would hear that for sure, I thought.

"OK! Let yourself down, Thump!"

I felt my feet touch Whitey's back. "Good! Now, just hang there from the window sill while I move out from under you." Before I could protest, Whitey edged out from under me. He grabbed me around my butt and pulled me away from the house. I didn't even touch the ground, because I was swooped around and thumped onto his bicycle seat. The dog leaped through the window and sailed to the ground with no effort at all. Whitey was so damn strong, and I wondered if that strength was part of his *gift*. He mounted the bike, and we were off down Bloom Street, past Mrs. Kinsolving's house. "We'll go there and check for *cats* some night!" Whitey wasn't whispering, because we were out of ear shot of anybody who cared. We hung a right, and we were on our way up Spirit Hill Drive toward the Woodard house. At the bottom of the road that went up there, Whitey stopped and held the bike up so it wouldn't fall. He just stood there, straddling the bar with his hands on the grips.

"Lookit that."

"What?"

"Up there in the sky ... straight ahead. It's Venus. The evening star. She's the first one out every night. Did you know that?"

"You mean STAR LIGHT, STAR BRIGHT, FIRST STAR I SEE TONIGHT? That one? My sis is always reciting that and making wishes about boys, but I never knew that star was called Venus."

"Yep. But its actually a planet." Whitey just kept looking ahead and gazing. "You're gonna always remember Venus is up there, Pal." He put his foot on the pedal, and we slowly headed up Woodard's lane. The sky was clear. Whitey had told me to pray for no clouds, and it worked. I was grateful for that later.

"I just remembered I left my crutch back at your house."

"Don't worry about it." We cruised past the Woodard front porch, around the house, past the barn, through the apple orchard and saw the tree house and Mr. Woodard. They were silhouetted in the dark red of the western sky. Mr. Woodard waved as we rode toward him.

"Almost nine o'clock! You're right on time."

"What does he MEAN, we're right on time? I don't even know why we're here! We're really gonna be in troub ..."

"Shhhh."

"Little Buddy, you have an appointment. That's why you're here." Mr. Woodard chuckled.

WHERE THE MONSTER DIED

16

CONNIE'S TWO CENTS WORTH

We're rolling into Whitey's driveway, and my friend is now asleep on my shoulder. The porch light is on, and Connie must have stayed up all night, because there she is standing in the doorway with her hands on her hips. I'm trying to assess the look on her face. I'm engineering my way out of the truck and trying to keep Whitey from falling sideways and hitting his head on the steering wheel.

"I think I could use your help getting your husband into the house." Connie is in her fuzzy, blue robe and slippers. She's not happy, and she is an intimidating person when she is worked up about something. All one hundred eighty pounds of her. She stops for a few seconds while she stares at the billowing, blue haze floating up from our cargo in the truck bed. I'm telling her that it isn't as bad as it looks, and that the plan went fairly well, almost until the last minute. Whitey is groggy and no help at all in the transfer from the truck to the house. He is being negotiated between us, as I tell Connie the plan about taking showers, changing clothes and going to emergency with a trumped up story about tripping over dogs and falling down stairs.

Connie helps me get Whitey into the bedroom, and we lower him onto the bed. "Could you fix us guys some breakfast while we get cleaned up, Babe? By the way, I think my ankle is broke." Whitey struggles to unbutton his coat. His hands are trembling, and he is a little blue in the gills. He gives me a look like we're probably in big trouble, because Connie has been extremely quiet. I'm reaching down to help him when Connie's plump hand comes down hard on my shoulder and stops all the action.

"Here's what's going to happen, boys." Connie is using her Drill Sergeant voice now. "Warren is going to take the damn truck home and figure out what to do with what's in it. He's going to take his shower at his own house and take care of his own crap. We'll figure out how to get the truck back here later. You, my crazy husband, are going to emergency with me, in my car … No shower, no nothin'. You let me do the talking. See you later, Warren, and drive carefully."

I'm thinking Connie's plan is much simpler.

17

STRAIGHTEN UP AND FLY RIGHT

"How you feelin' tonight, Mr. Warren Hearst?" Old Man Woodard asked me. Whitey's arms circled my waist and lifted me off the bike. He was real gentle as he put my feet on the ground.

I told him I was pretty good, but worried about what was going to happen if my parents found out I wasn't where I should be, since the rule at our house was to be inside when the street lights came on.

"It won't matter, Pal."

"You wanted to go up in the tree house, so let's get to it. Hop yourself over to the ladder, Thump."

It looked higher than it did the first time I saw it, somehow. Whitey could just BEAM me up there if he wanted to, but the little twerp didn't. It was the longest set of steps I ever climbed, and I got no extra help except a lot of encouragement from Mr. Woodard and my bossy friend. There were eight steps nailed to the tree trunk, and I had to stop and rest a couple of times on the way up. Whitey had already scurried up the ladder like a squirrel ahead of me and was talking me up all the way. I would step on my good leg; pull myself up with my arms to the next step. It reminded me of my very first trip up the stairs to my attic room at home. My bad leg just dangled and was no help at all. I was two steps from the entrance and almost out of breath when Whitey reached down for me.

"Take my hands." I was scared of falling but had to trust Whitey.

I flung my right arm up, and Whitey grabbed my hand. I forced myself to let go with my left hand, and my life was in the total care of Whitey Swift. I shot upward and was suddenly being pulled on my tummy across the floor of the house.

Samson barked. If a dog could say "Good boy!" Samson just did. Mr. Woodard scratched the pup's ears and came to the bottom of the ladder. "Think I'll just stand guard down here, fellas."

"That wasn't so bad now, was it, Thump? Gimme your hand." I was still on my belly, so Whitey pulled me up to a standing position.

I didn't know what was going on. I had wanted to go up in the tree house the first time Whitey brought me to the farm. I didn't understand why we had to wait and come up here in the dark.

"I want you to look out the window at something." Whitey's arm went around me to steady my pathetically tired body as I took a couple of hops to look at the view out the little window on the west side of the house. "See her? See Venus? She's yours tonight, Thump. It's the Warren Hearst Venus at this very minute, and nobody else's." I put my hands on the window ledge and looked out at the brightest planet that was outshining everything else in the sky except the moon which was just to the left of her and a little bit higher. It was a crescent moon, just looking at Venus and smiling.

"Don't move, just lookit her and think great thoughts and dreams, Buddy. Take a real deep breath and hold it for a couple of seconds." He squatted down and put his hands on my brace. It started to get warm and then even warmer.

"I'm not supposed to take that off."

"Keep looking at Venus." It was hard to keep looking at Venus when there was other traumatic stuff going on with Whitey and my brace. I heard a tiny sound like the sound of breath, then a louder, sizzling noise that seemed to come from Whitey's hands as they loosened the straps. My brace was getting real hot now, and I started to worry about burning my leg. The little house was full of glowing, white swirling clouds as Whitey pulled that cumbersome ball and chain from my useless leg. "Move a little to your left, Thump, but keep your eyes on

Venus." He flung my brace out the window. It sailed outward as if it had no weight. It was glowing blue and white and whirling. Then there was nothing. It never even hit the ground. It was gone. "Keep looking at Venus, Buddy, and keep thinkin' good stuff."

The clouds in the little house were whirling around like a tornado. Whitey was hanging on to me when the air turned so cold, it was hard for me to breathe. It was hard to keep my eyes open and hard to keep looking at that bright thing in the sky. My Venus. Then there was the roar, like that locomotive Whitey told me about less than an hour ago. It was nearly breaking our ear drums when those glowing clouds all raced out the window and fell to the ground like a water fall. I held on to the window ledge, shaking and trying to breathe. Then it was dead silent. Less than dead silent if that was possible. Whitey unlocked his arms from around my chest. I was breathing easy now.

"Does this m … magic show happen every t … time you c … come up here?" I was shaking so hard, it was a struggle to talk.

"No. This could be the last time this will happen for me. The first time I was up here I got the *gift*. This is the second time for me, and the last, probably. Each of us gets two times, Thump. One for himself and one for a *chosen*. Only *chosens* or *past chosens* can be here for this." Whitey's eyes were glowing like neon. They were brimming, and I wondered why. "I'm goin' on down, Pal. You take a few minutes up here by yourself."

"Aren't you gonna hang out up here for awhile?" I was still shaking and already worried about the trip down the ladder. I was still standing in the window and holding on to the sill to steady myself. I was confused and didn't understand the reason for the strange light show. Maybe I had been through some kind of initiation for a club."I'm gonna need help getting down from here!"

"You can stop standing on one leg now, Pal." Whitey yelled from the ground below.

I stood up there in the dark by myself. I still had my hands on the dumb old window sill just looking out at Venus. I'll never know where it came from, but I thought I heard a faint voice coming from the hills out west. "*It's all right now. You can let go, go, go.*" It echoed. Venus shimmered blue, then white again. Then a few thin clouds covered her up, like she had pulled down the shade for the night.

I could hear my own breath. It was slow, like I didn't know whether to keep breathing. I let my bad leg touch the floor, and when it did there was sound like a sigh. I remember noticing that I had no pain, and both legs looked and felt alike. I became suddenly brave and lifted my good leg off the floor. I was standing firm. I breathed faster and faster and started to shift weight from one leg to another like … *walking.* This turned into a march, and I let go of the window sill and, before I knew it, I was counting ONE TWO THREE FOUR as I marched in place on TWO good legs! I began to laugh, and tears were running down my face, while I marched in a circle up there on the floor boards of the tree house. I was singing LONDON BRIDGE is FALLING DOWN as I marched around in time with the beat of the music. Whitey and Mr. Woodard patiently waited down below me. When I looked down at them, my friends were smiling and looking up at me. I turned around and put my foot on the second step down. I pushed away from the tree trunk, skipped the rest of the steps and landed on the ground in a squatting position. Then I shot straight upright just like a Jack-in-the-box! "C'mon, Samson!" The dog and I raced around in a huge circle, leaping over rocks and logs and dodging around trees and skipping through the weeds. I finished this production with two cartwheels and wound up back where I had started … ahead of Samson. I realized that I was the *chosen* and, briefly, I thought ahead to a second time up in the tree house, where I would have picked a *chosen* and held that person around the chest as we gazed at Venus and stood in a whirlwind of clouds and magic and healing heat.

"You're driving *me* home, Pal." Whitey said. I eagerly threw my leg over the bar, and my buddy jumped onto the seat. Mr. Woodard gave us the high sign, and Samson raced down the road behind us.

18

THE SKIN OF OUR TEETH DISCUSSION

I have talked to Whitey a couple of times this week on the phone, and now Connie has given him permission to meet at Bucky's Place for coffee with me. She now has the upper hand, since Whitey is in a cast up to his knee and using crutches. It kind of gives me the willies when I think about it. He used to call me Thump, but somehow it doesn't seem too appropriate for me to try that with him. It's not in me. I have a white dressing on my head over my left eye with five stitches under it.

I'm wrestling Whitey's empty truck into the parking lot at the cafe, just as Connie slides in next to me in her new, green VW bug. Whitey looks less than happy all folded up in the passenger seat which is pushed back as far as it will go. Connie has made the plan for the return of Whitey's truck. I'm to bring Whitey home in the pickup, and Connie is driving me back home after that in the VW. She seems real bossy, but I know she only has Whitey's welfare in mind. I've known her long enough to know that. She's a great gal.

I help my pal out of the car and hand him his crutches that are in the back seat. We take longer than usual getting to the door of Bucky's Place, since Whitey is not too practiced with crutches. "Turnabout is fair play. Eh, *Thump?*"

"I don't think so." He looks pathetic.

I'm telling him about my visit to the Doc and how I had expected to get a Tetanus shot and a bandage but wound up with stitches, too.

"You almost look worse than I do."

"You boys sure would be exciting out on a date. Whatya havin?" Petty isn't asking any questions. She probably got the skinny from Connie and knows the poop already.

"Same as usual." Petty scuffs off with a smirk.

"How'd it go when you got the truck to your place?"

"I had my car out at the curb in front, so I ran the truck right into my garage. I left it there until morning. Too tired to do anything else. Slept most of that day after I saw the Doc. Had to put plywood over the garage windows, because when it got dark you could see the blue and white stuff shining out. I hope Wilber and Rose next door didn't notice that. I emptied the truck bed the next day and put the tarp back over the stuff, but it was still doing that weird, glowing thing and leaking out under the edges."

"It has a way of doing that. Always will until it gets reassembled again somewhere."

Our plates arrive, and we are quiet for a few minutes while we chow down. Whitey isn't asking me anything about my plans for the future of the tree house, and I'm not saying anything. We both know that there is a definite future, however. Sometime. It will be unsaid for now.

"I'm not gonna be much help ... whatever you're planning." Whitey is wearing his Coke bottle glasses. Age and being worn out does strange things to a person's vanity.

"I'm toying with the idea of putting it in the back yard, in that old Maple tree. Gotta put it up somehow. It's mine now. It's a sacred thing. I gotta do that to honor Old Man Woodard, don't you think?"

"He would be proud." Whitey is smiling at me and looking smack into my brain. I have always felt a little uncomfortable with that aspect him. "Gimme a little time, and we'll git her done. How 'bout April Fool's day? That ought to get me on the road to being useful to somebody, and Connie might let me off the dog leash by then." *Fart on a griddle. As always.* "The ankle is starting to throb,

Buddy. Think we better get me home to put my foot up. Not as tough as I used to be."

I picked up the tab, left Petty a tip, and we made our way to Whitey's pickup.

"I'll get the stuff organized in the garage, and in the meantime you pay attention to your wife. I'll keep in touch." I help him into the passenger side of his truck.

On the way to Whitey's house, I mention the fact that people were glancing at us in the cafe. "You don't think anybody knows what we did?"

"Just my wife and Petty. Might as well put it on the six o'clock news."

19

NICE GUYS FINISH FIRST

I was peddling Whitey's bike. We flew like the wind, but this time it was Whitey holding on to the waist of my blue jeans instead of the other way around. I hadn't had time to think any farther ahead than this very minute of living my most earnest dreams and prayers. I had come out of the darkest hole into the most golden, happy light. I thought that this had to be what heaven must be like. There was a god who must have heard me and loved me. I was a good boy, after all. Mom and Dad always told me I was a good kid, but I had begun to doubt it when Polio grabbed me and punished me. What had I done wrong to be slammed down that way?

I was peddling slower now, because there was a tiny, bothersome thought that started working in my brain. I brought the bike to a gradual stop about a block from Whitey's house.

"What're you doin'? We just got up to speed."

"I got to thinking about my folks and my sis. What am I gonna *tell* 'em?" Mum was the word when it came to explanations about things that happened to *chosens*. "What did you tell YOUR mom?" I deemed Whitey an expert.

"My mom doesn't know nothin'. She's never seen me in action, and she won't unless she's about to get killed by something, and I happen to be there. I would probably think of something real quick if I had to. Just don't worry about it, Pal. Your mom and dad are gonna be so happy, they'll *forget* to ask how it happened."

"No, they won't."

I wasn't even worried that Whitey's mom might catch us climbing through the bedroom window when we pulled up into the side yard. Nothing else seemed important except the fact that I wasn't a poor crip anymore. I wasn't going to be in pain anymore, and I wasn't going to have to put on a brace and carry a crutch. I WAS going to ride my bike, run, jump, wrestle with Whitey and maybe even beat him. I was excited about going to school in the fall instead of being a hermit living in a cave in the mountains. I wouldn't worry about peeing my pants because I couldn't get down the steps fast enough. I would play shortstop again. I would get my SCHWINN BLACK PHANTOM out of the garage and take it to Pete at the bike shop for a good going over. Yeah.

Whitey and I finally climbed into bed, followed by Samson who flew in through the window in slow motion. I knew that it wasn't going to be an overnight stay. I knew I couldn't sleep, and I would be practicing the speech I would have to tell Mom and Dad. It was about ten thirty when I reached down where Whitey was being real quiet lying on the floor on the living room sofa cushions. I tapped him on the shoulder.

"I'm not asleep. I know you're gonna go home now. I *get* it. I'd do the same thing, Thump ... I mean, Pal." I thanked my best friend, which didn't seem like enough. I had no problem slipping back out through Whitey's bedroom window and dropping to the ground all by myself.

I wasn't surprised that the front door to my house was locked, and the lights were out. I didn't want to bang on the door because it was going to be a big enough shock without that. I walked through the wet grass to the side where Beverly's bedroom window was, and I noticed her little bed light was on. Sis was probably looking at her glamour magazines and cutting out pictures of movie stars to put on her wall. She had them taped all around her dresser mirror like a big frame.

It was almost eleven o'clock, and I was glad to see some sign of life. I was just a little kid out in the dark at the wrong time and not where my parents thought I was. I decided to try my luck with Beverly, hoping she would help me break the news ... to hold me up a little bit when the wave happened. In a loud whisper I said, Beverly! Beverly! But she didn't hear me. I broke a branch from the lilac bush and began to slap it on the glass of her window. I was praying that she wouldn't get scared and yell for Mom and Dad. Then, I saw her peek through her pink curtain. Her eyes were huge, and I saw her lips move, like she was saying *Warren!* I mouthed, "*Open the front door!*"

She just stared down at me from her window for what seemed forever, and then she mouthed "*OK.*" I put my pointer finger over my lips to tell her not to make any noise and made my way back to the porch steps. I was getting cold and kind of shaking, and my socks felt damp and clammy, since I left Whitey's without my shoes.

The door swung open, and Beverly was all ready to tell me how much trouble I was in for being outside alone at that time of night. "Little Brother, how come you're out here so late all by yourself? You're lucky I was home. I didn't go to the slumber party. It got cancelled, because Patty got grounded …" She stopped and took in a big gulp of air and covered her mouth with her hands when it sunk in that I was without my crutch and my brace.

Where's your …"

"Gone."

"How did you get home without them?"

"I just … did." I knew what was coming next. My brain was racing.

Beverly took two very slow steps toward me and put her hands on my shoulders. I remember her bending down so that our faces were so close we could feel each other's breath.

"What HAPPENED, Warren? You're scaring me." There were tears in her eyes. This wasn't the big, smarty, teenage sis I knew.

"I don't know. I was looking at the stars, and I made a wish on Venus like you always did. Whitey was with me in his back yard when it happened. It's just a, a … **miracle**, I guess." I tried not to, but I started to cry and asked her if she please would go with me to wake up Mom and Dad.

"Oh, my God … Yes." She took my hand as if she was going to help me walk. I told her I guessed she wouldn't have to help me walk anymore.

"I'm not trying to help you, Little Brother. I just want to hold your hand, because I'm so happy." It felt a little awkward for me having my sis be so nice. But it was a good feeling.

We just stood there looking at each other for a couple of minutes. She hadn't let go of my hand. "Here's what we'll do, Kiddo." She put her arms around me real tight, and her mouth was right by my ear when she told me the plan. She kissed me on the cheek, which almost never would happen in normal life. Then she led me into the living room and left me standing there while she went to Mom and Dad's bedroom door. My knees were shaking like crazy.

I heard her whisper, "Mom, Daddy, Warren's *home.*" I heard the covers of their bed rustle, and Mom said "What in the world ...?" Dad commented on what time it was. They hurried into the living room while Beverly kept saying things like, "Don't worry, it's good. He's fine. You won't believe your eyes. Don't be mad. Wait'll you see ..."

I felt naked standing there with no hardware on my leg and no crutch. I started to smile at them just a little bit, just to let them know I was fine and that this was good news. Dad looked confused, and Mom just stood there with her hands over her mouth. I didn't know if I could handle that wave of realization and emotion that was about to happen. What I was about to do might hold off the wave for a minute or two. It was Beverly's idea, and I thought it was a good one. I lifted my good leg and slowly put it back down. Then, up came my BAD leg, and I started to march real slow, then faster and faster. I swung my arms and started singing Ten Little Indians. "Watch THIS!" I galloped through the dining room and around the table and took the steps up to my attic room two at a time and came back down those twelve steps in two seconds, NOT holding on to the railing. I even skipped the last three stairs and leaped to the floor. "Ta DAAAAH." I threw my arms up and did that victory dance that Rocky did at the top of the steps in the movie. I guess I invented it way before Sylvester did. I was pretty much out of breath by this time. Yep, I remember every detail, because the memory is part of the *gift!*

Mom collapsed to the floor on her knees with her arms out. "Come here, my Baby." She was sobbing. So was Dad, and he also came down on his knees next to Mom. I was sobbing right along with them now and didn't know why. Then

Beverly joined all of us, giggling and crying at the same time. There was none of our usual competition for attention now.

"Warren told me he wished on a star!" Bev blubbered and sniffed and wiped her face on the sleeve of her pajamas.

I hoped maybe I wouldn't have to answer any questions, at least for awhile. After all, I was too busy being smothered in hugs and kisses, and I wasn't thinking about any explanations.

"I think it's a miracle!" Beverly was helping my situation, big time. Then everybody got real quiet there in a bunch, kneeling on the floor with me standing in the center. It was like they didn't want that warm feeling to end. I just let that quiet stuff continue for a few seconds.

"I guess I can get my bike out now, can't I Dad?"

Mom started in again. "Oh, my Lord, Bernie! It's a spontaneous healing! There's just no other explanation! A SPONTANEOUS HEALING!"

I knew that there would be a million questions from my folks once all of this celebration was over. I also knew that Whitey would be at the center of all of them. I think, eventually they looked at Whitey as an angel sent just for me, even though I knew he really wasn't any angel! And I can tell you this … Mom and Dad and Beverly never looked at that little white-haired Beamshooter again in the same way.

WHITEY'S HOUSE

20

MY HEART BLEEDS

The soaking Sunday World Herald is spread all over the kitchen table and the floor. Damn thing slipped out of the orange, plastic sleeve when it hit the ground this morning. All 30 pounds of it. Barnabus is racing around and burrowing his nose under the pages and hiding in the paper tents he creates. Right now he has chosen the want ads.

Today, Wendy, Bernie and I are going to the buffet together, as we usually do on Sunday, barring unforeseen things like measles or tornadoes. I'm picking them up at 11:30. My stitches are gone from over my eye. I had told Wendy I slashed it working under the car. That excuse worked the first time with the doctor, and it worked with Wendy and Bernie. "YOU GOT A BAD OUCHIE." That was the Trooper's outdoor-voice assessment. Bernie patted it gently with his fat little hand. There will be a scar, I'm told. Whitey, of course, had to say something smart about how it'll make me look rugged and worldly for all the women in my life.

I have an hour to kill before I leave to pick up the kids, so I'm looking out the back porch at the Maple tree. I have a yellow pad and a pencil. The paper is blank so far, but I plan to do a preliminary sketch of what the tree house will look like in that lucky tree, that is, if I can quit losing sleep over whether this project should go forward. There's no question that the structure should be rebuilt. It's my legacy. I was the last one on that list carved into the wood. It's real strange, that lumber. It doesn't show any disintegration, even though the names on the ledger go back to 1924 when Old Man Woodard was probably middle aged, whatever that means. Perception of middle age has a way of readjusting as the years go by. I'm guessing that Woodard was probably the original *chosen*, but don't ask me who might have been the one to lead him up those ladder steps on a starry night in June a long time ago.

I haven't heard from Whitey for about a week, and I haven't bothered him either; but he isn't one to be able to sit still for very long. I'll be hearing from him soon, since he was the one to set April 1st for launching the project. That's only a couple of weeks away. His wife might put a brick wall in front of that early date if she diagnoses Whitey as NOT YET ABLE TO PARTICIPATE. That's how she would put it, I know her. That's pure Connie.

I'm in my only clean pair of Dockers, walking shoes, a flannel shirt and my wind breaker, hoping I don't freeze. The older I get, the less I can stand the chill of early spring or early anything. I'm gathering up the limp pages of the newspaper and stacking them flat on a rack in the oven, which I'm not turning on. That's one place where Barnabus can't get to it. He has his rations, and the TV is on for him. He'll be fine. He loves having the house to himself. I know this, because he always looks at me like I've interrupted a romantic encounter when I come home.

The car is warm when I pull up to the curb in front of Wendy's house. I give the horn a polite honk, and now Bernie is hurrying toward me. "HI, PAW PAW!" There's a big smile on his face, and his arms are both up in the air. His pudgy little hands are waving at his grandpa. He is wearing his bright red Husker hoodie and his SPECIAL OLYMPICS cap. "Crawl in the back and buckle up, Trooper." Wendy is setting the security alarm at the front door. She jogs to the car and slides into the front seat next to me and gives me a smooch on the cheek.

"FRIED CHICKEN AND PUDDING!" Trooper yells from the back seat.

"You got that right, Trooper!"

Wendy leans forward and looks around at my head. "Looks better, Daddy."

"You outta see the other guy." That's what I always say. She expects it. She's rolling her eyes and faking a big yawn.

On the way to the Super Duper Buffet, I notice some boys skate boarding on the sidewalk in the rain. I worry about the dangers of skate boarding, but I also have that little thing in my head that says it would be great to see Bernie doing the fancy maneuvers in a skate park. Wendy sees the boys, too.

"I GONNA GET A KATE BOARD, TOO."

Someday, Trooper."

"Don't I wish." Wendy says quietly.

We small talk the rest of the way to Super Duper. We're beating some of the after church crowd, so we're on our way home by one o'clock.

"Can you come in for awhile, Daddy? I'll make you a cup of coffee. Bernie Bern and I will have a long afternoon stuck inside, and you and I haven't had a good visit for awhile." Wendy's eyes look like they might well up. I hate that. She seems so at sea sometimes, even though I try to be positive when I'm with her and encourage her. It's all I can do not to get started mentally killing Dr. BIRD DOG who walked out on them in K.C. I had brought my daughter and her baby home with nothing but some diapers, and Wendy took her maiden name back.

"Sounds good to me."

The Trooper takes off his Husker hoodie and his cap and puts them in his bedroom. I throw my jacket over a kitchen chair while Wendy makes the coffee. "Want to watch cartoons for a while, Bernie Bern?" She turns on the TV in the living room. Bernie jumps on to the sofa, and he's holding his brown Teddy bear. "I got Boo Boo, MaMa."

"Good for you, Bernie Bern.!" Wendy tells me to sit at the kitchen table. "Want a little something in it?" She grabs some rum out of the cupboard and is pouring a generous amount into her mug. I decline, because it's a little too early in the day for me. This kind of disturbs me. I've never seen her do this, but like I have said before, I'm not in on every aspect of my daughter's life. She pours the coffee into the mugs and tops hers off with some sugar and milk along with the rum.

I'm watching her put the booze back into the cupboard, and she has her back to me. She's slumped over with her palms on the counter. She's just standing there with her head down. "Wendy?" I go to her. She turns to me and buries her face in my chest and puts her arms around me. I'm holding her. What else would I do?

"I'm so tired, Daddy. I feel guilty saying it."

We are just quietly standing in the middle of the kitchen. I can hear the rain. I'm thinking that the sky is crying, too. I'm thinking of my parents back in '49 when I was one sick little puppy and how it must have been for them. My mother must have cried just like this with her face on my father's chest. But that was only temporary. It had and end. I got well.

"You need some rest, Sweetheart."

"I'm taking some days off work around the first of April. That'll help. Bernie Bern will be gone during the day, and I can have some time for just me, but I feel so dreadfully selfish."

"You're not selfish, Sweetheart. Trooper is better off, too, when you're rested! He can come to my house for a slumber party one night during that week. We'll have hot dogs, and popcorn."

By the time I'm leaving her house and giving hugs to my favorite people in the world, Wendy is able to reward me with a little smile. I have given her a small shot in the arm, just like a dad should do.

"You want to come stay over night with Grandpa?" I'm getting hugged.

"SHOW ME HOW TO KATE BOARD!"

"He watches the Olympics when they're on, and football and basketball, Daddy. He tries to be just like the athletes, and he copies all their moves. Why shouldn't he want to KATE board?"

"You betcha. Why shouldn't he?"

One more hug, and I am on my way home. The sun is trying to show itself through a space in the dark clouds. It's after three now, and there is a rainbow in the east as I'm wheeling into my driveway. I can't quit thinking that my grandson has yearnings. I'm always wondering if he is a real happy kid, or if he knows what he will never be able to do somewhere down deep in his challenged mind. I love him more than life, just the way he is. He is who he is … but I wish he could skate board. I remember those weeks when my bike was stashed out in the garage and I was in bed.

I unlock the side door into the kitchen, and I hear a solid thump of a cat dropping off the kitchen table. Instead of feeding Barnabus immediately, I call Whitey.

"Can you talk Connie into bringing you over to my place tomorrow morning for awhile? I'll make the coffee, and you can get a look at the lucky Maple tree."

"You bet, Buddy Boy. Connie has been drivin' me nuts anyway."

"Nine thirty OK?"

"Yep." Click.

21

BEHIND THE EIGHT BALL

I'm reading the USA TODAY when Connie wheels into the drive and noses her green VW to within about one inch of the back of my car. I haven't organized the garage yet, so the Buick is still out. I hurry to get outside so I can be of some help getting Whitey out of the car. Turns out, I didn't have to break my neck being helpful.

"She wouldn't bring me here in my own damn truck! There y'go." He hands me a box of bear claws. My guess is that he wants to stay as long as I'll let him. What surprises me is how fast he is able to get himself out of the bug, stand on one leg and grab his crutches from the back seat and be ready to roll.

"Stay out of trouble." Connie wings out of the driveway. I'm guessing that their time alone together in the house is wearing thin.

"I'll bring him home!" She gives me the OK sign.

"Take your time!"

Whitey chooses the kitchen table over a soft chair in the living room, and Barnabus leaps up and sits on the box of bear claws and starts licking his butt. I'm scooping coffee into the basket.

"What's the plan, Buddy?"

"Just starting to figure out the construction details."

"Somethin' on your mind?"

"Yeah, there is." I turn on the pot and sit down across the table so I can talk to Whitey eye to eye. "Except for me, you're the only *chosen* around here, right?"

"Unless your kitchen is full of their ghosts."

"Well, it has to do with the *next* chosen. What if the *family* of the chosen doesn't want the gift? You can't *ask* them, because you can't *tell* them about it, dammit! I remember those rules, and that's what's bothering me."

Whitey gently lifts Barnabus off the box of bear claws and helps himself to one of the gooey rolls. He's stuffing half of it, which probably has cat hair in the frosting, into his mouth. The whole time, he's just smiling as he chews. Those pink eyes are doing that *thing* again while he's maneuvering the wad of dough around with his tongue.

"Oo got a 'apkin?" I get him a couple pieces of paper towel, and I'm mildly irritated with him, because it's taking him forever to answer me. I pour the coffee into the mugs and carry them to the table.

He finally swallows, sucks the leftovers from between his teeth and wipes his mouth and hands before he talks to me. "Part of the *gift*, Pal, is the *remembering* part. If you think real hard, you'll remember what I told you back in 1949 when you were worrying about what you would tell your folks. I'm surprised at you WARREN." There was that damn whiney voice again that used to make me so mad, and it still does … only difference is that now the voice is lower and my neck cords don't stand out as much.

"Just refresh my old mind." I stuff a big bite of bear claw into my boca.

"They'll be so happy, they'll forget to ask how it happened. I'm surprised you didn't remember that, Pal! It was damned important! Part of the gift is that those it affects can't be *mad*! It's *part* of the *gift*! What kind of gift would it be if it made people mad?"

"But in this case it would mean taking some things away from the *chosen*. There would be a change, almost to a different person! What if his moth …"

"It's your grandson. I've always known that, Pal! Just do it! Think of what it would mean for Wendy and for Trooper! No doubts, Buddy. You gotta do it. You were the last *chosen,* and Trooper is next. A no-brainer."

I know I have to trust Whitey, and it goes both ways. He trusts me, too. After all, I am the only other person in this world who knows the truth about his monster father and those bloody railroad tracks.

◆   ◆   ◆

As we're slurping coffee and chomping on bear claws, we agree that my maple tree will accommodate the house. We decide that Venus can be seen, even though there are other trees around, and Whitey tells me that the house doesn't have to be exactly like it was before we tore it down and crashed right along with it into the bed of his truck.

"We just have to use the original wood. How is it behaving?" It takes me a minute to understand what Whitey means.

"The wood? Oh yeah, the wood. Well, it's still glowing like hell at night."

"It'll do that 'till we git 'er put together again."

"It'll have to be plenty sturdy with a good strong ladder. The Trooper's a hefty little guy, and we really have to be careful with him going up the ladder. He's got a problem with some vertebrae in his neck, and we just CAN'T have an accident, Buddy. He's twelve now, and he's starting to get some heft on him. He's a little awkward and can't see too well, either. I hope the kid isn't as accident prone as his grandpa."

"Are you done? Those *negatives* are the reason we're takin' Trooper up there!"

He has a point.

Whitey doesn't seem anxious to get back to his top sergeant, so I suggest that we migrate to the living room and some softer furniture. Whitey winds up in my recliner with his feet up. Barnabus makes himself comfortable on the back of the chair, purring into Whitey's ear. I can't help noticing those two pairs of eyes.

Feline and "humine". I'm seeing clear into their brains right now. Must be the position of the sun, or something.

"Back in the day, we wouldn't just be sittin' here, would we?"

"Not young anymore. Too tired, too stiff, too everything." I say.

"I keep busy with the grand kids, though. There's always some swim meet or ball game. Gotta be there. We're the grandparents, you know, Pal. Too bad my ma didn't live long enough to get in on some of that stuff."

"Not every kid can say they had a State Champion Wrestler for a grandpa." I remember how strong Whitey was then, still is. Reason nobody could pin him was his claustrophobia. Somebody try to restrict his movements, he'd panic. Quick as a rattle snake.

"I was wrestling when I met Connie. She was always on the sidelines lookin' at me. I thought she was just curious about my HYPO PIGMENTATION, but she told me it was my good looks. I didn't have to wear my glasses when I was wrestling, so I musta been quite a lady killer when I was on the mats. Yep, that was it, for sure. That was about the time I lost the Mutt."

I remember that day. Samson always slept in a clothes basket with a blanket in the bottom, and one morning he didn't get up for his breakfast. That was it. There he was, all curled up in there. Whitey buried him in the back yard right in that basket along with his blanket. He laid a tarp over him and covered it with dirt. His mom planted tulips on top, and they came up every year to remind us all. We loved that dog, and I sure missed him. Still do. You remember, he was special. He got some of the magic from Lady Venus. Old Man Woodard gave Whitey that dog.

"That dog helped save my butt on the playground."

"Saved both of us."

Whitey and I went to Omaha Tech High. He liked working with wood and building things, and I was into mechanical stuff, fast cars. In high school, Whitey was lettering in wrestling while I was drag racing in my spare time. We both graduated from Omaha University with degrees in business. I met Gwen in college. We were married the same year that Whitey and Connie were, and we were best man at each other's weddings. We've been down a lot of roads together. Whitey was at my side in the hospital when Gwen was fighting for her life. We tried to come up with a way to get her to the tree house, but it was just too late, and impossible under the circumstances. It still haunts me that we couldn't come up with a way to make Gwen my *chosen*, but I know she would have gladly sacrificed herself to give the Trooper a chance. Hope she's looking down here at my efforts.

Whitey suddenly looks at his watch. "Connie's probably gonna send the sheriff after me, Buddy." He pulls the lever on my recliner, and his feet hit the floor. In less than ten seconds, Whitey's standing and clumping toward the door. It's like the telephone. When Whitey's through talking, he hangs up. "I'm thinkin' we'll get this project done a lot sooner than planned. No reason to wait around if we don't have to. If my pesky leg isn't out of the cast, you can do the apprentice carpenter work, and I'll supervise from terra firma." The fart is still on the griddle.

I'm now dropping my partner in crime off at his house. He's getting more mobile, so I don't help him. I understand that *independence* thing. Been there.

"I'm shootin' for about a week from today. That's next Monday."

"Wednesday is Kiwanis, Friday is my haircut and Sunday is dinner with the kids. Monday's OK. This time we're gonna work in the daytime so we can see what the hell we're doing."

"You betcha." Whitey opens his door, slips out and grabs his crutches from the back seat. He is now hopping two times on his good leg before he plunks the crutches down, speeding his progress up to three times what it was when he first crashed out of the tree house. It reminds me of how fast I had streamlined my trips down the stairs from my attic when I was ten and in my brace with my own little crutch.

22

NO LIFE OF RILEY

It's Wednesday, and I'm just pulling into the drive after Kiwanis. My stomach is full of egg plant parmesan. Same menu every week, pretty much. My plans for the rest of the afternoon are to get out of these clothes, into a sweat shirt and jeans, and dabble around in the garage. The lumber is just like it was when I flung it all out of the truck that night after the tree disaster. I also plan to give Whitey a call tonight to confirm Monday.

Barnabus is trying to convince me it's supper time by sitting on top of the refrigerator like a vulture and glaring down at me. I'm in the kitchen out of habit even though my stomach is full. I give in and grab the cat treats and shake the box. Barnabus drops from his perch, hits the kitchen table and bounces on down to the floor in less than one second. "THREE! That's IT" I drop two more treats down. He runs my home life.

It's still chilly outside. Late March can be cold in Nebraska. I grab my zipper sweatshirt with the hood and head for the back door just as the phone rings. I'm thinking it's probably Whitey, since he always gets the jump on me when it comes to calling about something. But it isn't Whitey.

"Daddy?" This is not normal. Wendy is usually at work this time of day, and she doesn't sound right.

"Yeah, Sweetheart? What's going on?" I'm uneasy in the pit of my stomach.

"Oh, Daddy, I'm so worried. Bernie is in the hospital. He woke up with a temp of 102 this morning, and his cough sounds like a barking dog. I've been watching him real close for a couple of days. I thought it was just a cold, but I took him to the doctor this morning. He was wheezing so badly, and he was so

112

cranky. The doctor took a chest X-ray and says its pneumonia. He didn't even give us a choice about admitting Bernie immediately. I don't know how long he'll be here. I'm in his room right now. He's hooked up to an IV, and he gave them quite a fight. It wasn't pretty, and it's just not fair."

"I'll be right there, Honey." I can hear Trooper crying and coughing in the background. He doesn't like those damn needles. Neither do I.

23

MAÑANA AIN'T SOON ENOUGH FOR ME

It's about three o'clock, and I'm trying to speed the elevator up on my way to the Trooper's room in the children's wing of the hospital.

Wendy meets me outside the door and throws her arms around my waist. We're just standing here, holding each other. "It's been a bad day, Daddy. He's sedated now, thank God. The little guy screamed bloody murder and fought them. I couldn't watch anymore. He's drowsy now. Come on in." Trooper's little eyes are almost closed.

"His cheeks are flushed." I feel sick to my stomach.

"He's got a fever. I was going to stay here all night, but the nurse says I should get some sleep. Sleep. What a joke."

"I think the nurse is right, Honey. They'll take good care of him. They're used to this stuff." *Who can get used to this stuff?*

"But, he's going to wake up, Dad! What's going to happen when he finds out I'm not here? Remember the last time?"

"You have to be realistic, Sweetheart. You can't help him if you're not OK, yourself. Let's you and I go to the cafeteria for a little bite to eat. You need a break. Trooper's asleep. OK? We'll come back and see Trooper for a while after supper, and then I'll take you home. Leave your car here, and I'll bring you back in the morning."

Wendy is sitting on the edge of the bed, blowing her nose. Her eyes are wet and red. "OK, Dad. You're probably right." She suddenly sobs convulsively, and that just about does it for me.

"You know I'm here for you, Sweetheart." I'm now blowing my nose, too.

◆　　　◆　　　◆

It's Thursday, a little after five AM. I'm awake before the alarm, and haven't sleep worth a damn. I'm picking up Wendy at six thirty. Barnabus has had an extra early breakfast and a few scratches behind his ears from his room mate. My morning pills are slushing around in my empty stomach with my OJ, so I grab a couple of soda crackers. A sweet roll and hospital coffee will have to do, later. Wendy's front door is open, and she already has her jacket on when I drive up.

"Mornin', Daddy." It is quiet in the car all the way to the hospital.

"Bernie had a spotty night's sleep, and I had to convince him that I was the Good Fairy a couple of times, Ms. Hearst."

The nurse seems good with Trooper. It is the children's wing, though, so I would think that should be a prerequisite. I'm noticing that Trooper's Teddy bear has a bandage on his head. "Boo Boo fell out of bed and hurt his head." Trooper's voice is husky.

Wendy is kissing his head and his nose, and she's smiling bravely. I'm getting my turn, now.

"When you get rid of this old "bug", Trooper, we'll have to go fishing. You be a good boy and do what they say and get well real quick for Paw Paw!"

"I a good boy, Paw Paw. Boo Boo Bear is good, too. Can we go home now?"

"Soon as the doctor says it's OK. It won't be long!" Wendy is smiling, bravely.

"How's Bernard, this morning?" The doctor is coming through the door. He's real brisk, like a gust of wind. Trooper is looking suspiciously at a man who would call him Bernard.

The doctor looks at me, and Wendy quickly says, "This is my dad, Warren Hearst." We shake hands. The doctor listens to Trooper's heart and quickly scans Trooper's chart, as if he has already seen a million of them this morning.

"I see that Bernard got rid of some congestion during the night. I'll drop back in before the day is over. By then, we should have a better idea about when this little guy can go home, but we have to get those lungs clearing out first." Doc is gone in a flash. It pays to get to the hospital early.

I'm looking at my watch every twenty minutes, and fifteen minutes is three hours long. My daughter and I manage to finesse our way out of Trooper's room long enough to grab a bite of breakfast, and later, a pre-wrapped hospital sandwich with a Coke. Most of this time we're in Trooper's room. That's where we just have to be, that's all. I go down the hall and call Whitey at one point. He's making me call him back as soon as I get back home, no matter what time it is. Whitey is a pal, through thick and thin.

Wendy and I spend the afternoon, hovering around Trooper. He is sipping 7-Up through a straw, which isn't easy for him. The TV is on, and we're trying to find things that might grab his attention. Nothing really does the trick. I have read The Pokey Little Puppy to him twice. Thankfully, he is getting used to the nurses and doesn't think they're monsters from Mars anymore.

Its five thirty now, and Wendy and I are sitting across from each other at a table in the cafeteria. We're eating French dip sandwiches and green beans, which is mildly better than what we ate at noon in the snack bar. Nothing seems to taste very good when you're worried sick.

"He's been through just about enough, wouldn't you say, Daddy?"

"Yep. Been through enough."

"Surgery for that little hole in his heart. Doesn't remember that, thank God. Too little."

"Yep. Then that intestinal problem."

"I don't know what I would have done without you, Daddy. I would have been so alone."

"If I ever see that EX of yours again, I'm gonna ..."

"Don't go there, Dad. It doesn't help anybody, especially me."

We're sitting in Trooper's room now, waiting for him to get drowsy. The nurse is telling us we might as well go home for some rest. "I don't think he'll be awake very long, will you, Pumpkin?"

"Not seepy. I not goin' to seep for a long time." But Trooper is sleepy, and in a matter of minutes, he is zoning out on us. Wendy and I kiss our little man and slip out. She decides to take her own car home this time, so we part ways in the parking lot.

I'm watching her tail lights go around the bend, when I see a pickup truck pull in near my car down the row a few slots. It's Whitey. He's down to one crutch now, traveling with a little hop-step action, and he doesn't say anything until he is standing square in front of me.

"How you doin', Buddy?" He pats me on the shoulder.

This is a surprise visit, and I'm real glad to see Whitey. "I'm OK, but I'm worried about Wendy. She's pretty down."

"Understandable. Connie tried to tell me it wasn't the best time for me to take off half-cocked like this, but you know me. I'm driving with just one damn foot ... the wrong one. Connie's madder'n hell at me. How's our little guy?"

"Yeah. I know you, Pal. Trooper has had a rough time, and I think it's going to take dynamite to get his lungs cleared out. It's a slow process. He coughs until he gags and throws up. I've seen him this way before. It's about his third or fourth time with this nasty crap."

"Can we go up there now?" Whitey's eyes are drilling mine, which means he's on a bent. I know my answer has to be a yes, even though it's past visiting hours. In my opinion, there are no limited visiting hours when it comes to sick kids.

"If we go in through EMERGENCY, we can get up there. I don't think they'll say anything to us."

"They won't." Whitey begins his hop-step toward the building. It's a challenge for me to keep up with him, especially when he gets a thing going on in his mind. It's always been that way, even after I got rid of the Polio and could hold my own. A fart on a griddle, still.

"You're lookin' tired, Buddy." The elevator stops with a tiny bounce.

We reach room 211, and Whitey stops short of Trooper's door. The nurse comes out and looks at us kind of funny. I don't know why I'm feeling like I have to explain everything, but I try. Pathetically. "This is Whitey Swift. He's family. His plane just landed, and he's anxious to see the Trooper. He'll only stay a minute."

Whitey winks at her, and she returns the smile. "I'm Leslie. I'll be with Bernard for the night shift. Does he have a nickname?" This nurse is smarter than Doctor "Flash", who didn't take the time to ask about Trooper's preference of names.

"His nickname is Trooper."

"Thanks." She smiles, and she is noticing Whitey's pink eyes, which are following her.

"*Sweet*." Whitey watches her go out the door.

The only light in Trooper's room is what comes in from the hallway. Whitey moves toward the bed and lays his crutch across the foot. Trooper is asleep, but his breathing is noisy. The IV drip is doing its thing. "We won't stay too long, Pal. I know it's late, and I don't want to rile him up." He signals me to sit down in the only chair in the room. I'm situated right next to the head of the bed, so I can see Whitey's face. His eyes are like neon orbs, just as I saw them long ago in my childhood attic room.

Whitey cautiously sits on the edge of the bed, trying not to disturb the Trooper. His big, strong hands rest on the top of Trooper's head and those pink eyes are not more than a few inches from Trooper's face. Whitey's soft voice doesn't wake up our boy.

"We're gonna have some fun, aren't we?" His big palms are framing Trooper's face, holding it gently. "You're warm, my little friend." Whitey's hands move to the side of Trooper's head where his ears would be if he were someone else, but he isn't someone else. He's Trooper, and his tiny ears are a little lower. Whitey's hands move down and are cupping Trooper's ears like muffs. "Even your little ears are warm, aren't they, Buddy?" Whitey softly puts his pointer finger on Trooper's mouth and traces it all the way around his lips. Trooper's thick, little tongue is resting on his lower lip ... his normal look. "That tongue is gonna get a lot busier, Buddy." I have to strain to hear him. Whitey's hands move down to Trooper's neck, feeling the glands on the side. "I can feel your pulse beating, Little Guy. It's real strong. You know how it sounds? Ka blunk, Ka blunk. Ka blunk."

Whitey smiles, accentuating his crow's feet. He seems to be *willing* that persuasive stuff into Trooper to get well. I'm standing up now, because I just have to see Trooper's face. There is a slight smile there, even though he's asleep. Whitey places each of his thumbs on one of the little, closed eyes that have that extra fold of skin over the lid. "They're gonna see a new world, Pal." Whitey's big, rough hands take Troopers little, soft ones and bring them up together. Two little hands with double-jointed fingers inside two big, rough ones. "You gotta get well, Buddy. Be tough. Mama, Paw Paw, Whitey and Connie all love you." Whitey's hands gently lay down Trooper's little ones. He's patting Trooper's legs and touching those little square feet with the space between the big toe and the rest. "This little piggy went to market." He doesn't finish the rhyme, but smiles and kisses each toe. "He's a real gift, my man. Without *any changes*."

I'm doing my best not to get emotional, but I'm failing. I watch, as Whitey stands and picks up his crutch. He cocks his head as a signal for us to get going. It's almost eleven now. Once again, we're floating down in the quiet elevator. My friend walks slower now, like a show of respect for what Trooper has been through. We're getting closer to his pickup and my Buick.

I walk Whitey around to his door, in case he needs help. He tosses his crutch into the passenger seat, not needing me, it seems. "Get some rest, Pal. I can't have you droppin' out on me. I want you to go see that little guy of yours in the morning and plan to do an all-nighter with me tomorrow in your back yard. We can't wait. Every time he gets that pneumonia, he's weaker. It's bad stuff."

I feel like I'm sinking, and I'm wondering what Whitey sensed when he was having his private time with Trooper. Being the worrier I am, I have to question the timing for the Trooper's special appointment. "Are you sure this will work *now*? All the rest of the *chosen* were in the tree house in *June!* Isn't that the rule for …?"

"Doesn't have to be June, Pal. All you really need is Venus lookin' at you through the window. It's OK. I've been checkin' her out all along. I'll be at your place at noon, and I'll bring you a hamburger. See you tomorrow."

Whitey never changes, and if I was ever having any doubts about making Trooper my *chosen*, they're all gone.

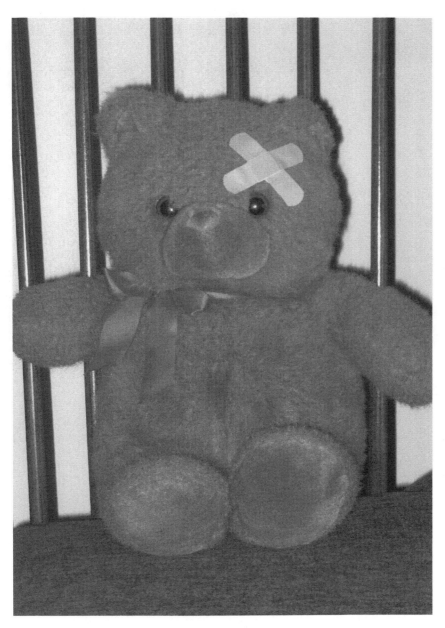

BOO BOO BEAR

24

STAIRWAY TO THE STARS AND FAST FOOD

Whitey isn't a healer. Wish he were, because if that were so, the Trooper would be well this morning. Whitey is a persuader, a motivator, and a person can't even get started to argue with him. He just *does that thing*. Ask Yours Truly. I watched as my pal talked and touched his way over my sleeping little Trooper last night. It was almost like he was *infusing*, or passing on an ability to *receive* whatever good might come. I saw my friend slow down and be gentle and patient and deliberate, instead of flying by the seat of his pants. It makes me uneasy when I think of what Whitey would be capable of doing, if his gift could be used willy nilly and at random. But it can't, which is a damn good thing. What if he got into the White House? 'Nuf of that wishful speculation on my part.

The sun is out this morning, and the wind is down. I got a fairly good night's sleep, so I feel I may be up for the task of the day. I'm pulling into the parking lot of the hospital, and I can see Wendy's car. It's almost nine, and I'll bet my daughter has been here for at least two hours already.

I'm coming in the door to Trooper's room when a booming voice yells, "BOO BOO IS ALL BETTER PAW PAW. ESWEE TOOK HIS BANNICH OFF! THEE?" That tiny little mouth is wide open and that fleshy tongue is lying on that lower lip. He's holding his Teddy bear up in the air by the ear. Wendy is smiling and drinking coffee in the chair next to the bed. Trooper's eyes are brighter today, and he's looking a lot better.

"Hi, Daddy! Quite a difference, wouldn't you say?" Wendy looks a little more rested too, and I give her a kiss on the cheek before I respond to that miraculous cure of Boo Boo. "Bernie Bern had a busy night, according to Leslie. I guess the meds he's getting sort of kicked in, and he spent a lot of time coughing up gunk out of his lungs and throwing up in the pan. She told me his fever broke about four this morning. She's off duty now, but I wish she would never get tired and could just stay. She's so good with kids. And mothers!"

"You seen the Doc yet?"

"I got here at six thirty, so, yes. I saw him. Says if things progress as he hopes, the kid here can maybe go home tomorrow. Depends on what happens today. He also told us that Boo Boo was all well and could go home, too! I was glad to see a sense of humor! We're planning a walk down the hall, too, aren't we Bernie Bern? Gotta get those lungs working and move the bad stuff out faster!"

"I can RUN FAST. Can Eswee run wif us?"

"No, little guy. Leslie had to go home and rest. She's been too busy with you all night, and she's all tired out!"

What a relief. Things are looking up at the moment, and I'm taking this opportunity to tell Wendy that I have some things to do today, so I won't be able to have lunch with her and the Trooper. Of course, I wouldn't bail out on them if things hadn't improved like they apparently have. "Whitey needs some help with a project this afternoon, and I said I would help. Whattya think, Sweet-heart?"

"Don't worry, Daddy. We'll be fine! It'll be good for you! Besides, I can always get you on your cell phone if you TURN THE DARN THING ON! What IS the project, by the way?"

I was afraid this was coming. "I, I'm … gonna help him stack some wood."

The day nurse is coming in now, and she says it's time for Trooper to take a short walk. Her name is Julie, and I'm wondering how she passed her boards. She is calling Trooper "Dream Boat." Trooper smiles. It seems to me that they are connecting on some level.

We get the little guy all untangled from the sheet and the IV pole around to the exit side of the bed. They're always on the wrong side when you need to get up. Wendy is on one side of Trooper, and I'm on the other. Nurse Julie is guiding the pole. Too many cooks, I'm thinking. "I can't keep up with you, Dream Boat!" Trooper's wide, little feet slap across the floor. I'm waiting to hear her say something without the name "Dream Boat" in it. She has a permanent, surprised look on her face like somebody just whacked her over the head with an iron skillet. Wendy is giving me a look. Can't describe it, but I understand it.

The walk has been uneventful, but good for Trooper. He didn't get to run like he wanted, but I can tell he's had enough walking as we're coming back into his room. That little side-to-side, flat-footed gait is quite a bit slower as we arrive at his bed. We're getting him all settled, when Nurse Julie says, "How about a nice big glass of soda, Dream Boat?"

Trooper is smiling at her, and his eyes are looking happy. He seems to like her, and that counts for a lot with a sick kid in a hospital. Soda? I haven't heard many people use that term in Omaha. I'm holding back on my assessment of Nurse Julie, because she might be just the ticket for the Trooper today. Maybe they're soul mates. Go figure.

I'm taking the opportunity to leave just as Trooper's lunch is brought in. "Bernie Bern says it's OK for me to go down to the cafeteria for my lunch, Daddy. I'll ride the elevator down with you."

"Gimme a kiss, Pal." I get a sloppy one on my cheek. "I'll see you later!"

"Bye Bye Paw Paw. See you 'morrow." Wendy and I hop on the elevator.

"Julie draws her eyebrows on way, **way** too high, and she RATS her bangs! It's sooooooo eighties! That's the reason for the vacant, stunned look, Dad." It's good to see Wendy think something is funny for a change. I'm wondering what "rat" means.

◆　　　◆　　　◆

I'm hauling the Buick out of the lot and hoping that the upcoming job won't really take all night. It's eleven forty-five when I pull into my driveway, and there's already a pickup truck in it. Whitey opens his window. "I'm gettin' good at drivin' with my left leg. Does that make me ambi<u>foot</u>ious?"

"Spose so. You sure you should be driving like that?" Whitey's right leg is sticking straight out to the right with his foot on the floor of the passenger side.

"I got tired of being chauffeured all over the damn town. It's a little tricky with the left leg doing the peddles. Got 'em mixed up on the way over to the hospital last night and shot through a red light like a Roman candle, when I hit the gas instead of the brake. Everything feels a little inside out. Don't tell Connie about that. She didn't want me to drive, and she's madder'n hell."

Whitey is back to his old self today after the transformation I saw in Trooper's room last night. I shouldn't have been surprised at his sensitivity. I believe I have already mentioned that he and Connie raised eight kids and have eighteen grandchildren.

Whitey passes our lunch through the truck window. It's Runzas and French fries. I ask him if he wants some coffee, and he says he's on the wagon. "Makes me too wired. How about a beer?" I'm not thinking that's a good idea so early.

"I have beer, but it's not cold. I'll put it in the refrigerator, and it'll be OK for later when we'll appreciate it more." Probably as a pain killer if there's another incident like the last one out at the Woodard place.

We make our way into the kitchen, and I drop the sack on the table. Whitey isn't using the crutch now. He's doing the "gallop" by stepping heavily on his left leg and very lightly on the right. I'll let you imagine it, since my sound effects are not adequate. We're having a Coke in a cold can, and Whitey is ignoring the fact that Coke is as bad as coffee when it comes to wiring up a person. Barnabus is in the center of the table with his head inside the Runza sack.

"Whattya think, Buddy Boy? I move we get goin'." Lunch is gone, and Whitey's right. I'm not looking forward to working through the night on this project. It is one thing to demolish a structure in the dark, but it's another thing to build one. "I figure since the tree is so close to your garage, we'll just make the ladder go up the side of the building, then put a connecting walkway from there to the tree. There's only a couple of feet on up to the fork, so one or two more boards on the tree, and we got it. We start from the bottom up. Make sense?"

"Yeah, sort of."

My ladder suggestion goes down the toilet after we discuss the peaked roof and the construction of a flat walkway. It's back to the old foot holds right up the trunk. The KISS method. *Keep it simple, stupid.*

"We gotta have some two-by-fours for the base anchor and the uprights. There has to be a stable level all around the tree, and then we can lay the original wood on top of it.

"Criminey. I wish I'd thought of that. I didn't know we could mix any other wood with the original stuff."

"I don't really know that for a fact. But the damn TREE ain't the original stuff, and it's got a whole different configuration. We gotta start from scratch on the blue prints. You got any old wood in the garage? Maybe up in the rafters?"

"No, dammit. Just fishin' poles, about fifteen of 'em."

"I have some lumber." We both turn our heads toward Wilber's house, and there he is in his driveway with his hands in his pockets, looking at us. Sometimes street supervisors aren't a bad thing.

"What are you fellas doing, if I may ask? Just curious, y'know."

I don't know what I was thinking, when I planned on putting this thing up without anybody noticing it. Whitey is grinning up a storm. He has his protective sun glasses on, and Wilber can't see Whitey's eyes. I'm glad about that.

"We're building a tree house for my grandson, and it's a surprise." I introduce him to Whitey.

Wilber has a skeptical look on his face, and I'm thinking we're in for it. "You plan to paint the thing?" He's just staring up at the tree, and I'm positive he's not happy about an eye sore back here.

"No, we're not."

"You don't want to paint a tree house! It's a HIDEAWAY! It's a FORT! It's PRIVATE! It has to BLEND. Young bucks don't want the whole world to know where they hold their meetings and make plans and have secrets and keep others out! You don't want to paint it! If it was MINE, I'd be up there all the time! I get tired of cleanin' things in the house. It would be a wonderful getaway! Rose comes up with one darn thing after another for me to do! Wish I was a kid again. Don't *paint* it."

"We were thinkin' the same thing." Whitey says. He's quick.

"I'll get you some two-by-fours. How many?" Wilber is definitely on board with the project.

"I think we'll need around ten." Whitey says.

Wilber turns and marches to his garage. I tell Whitey that I'll help Wilber, and Whitey just grins like the cat that got the cream.

Wilber Swan's garage is literally lined with shelving made with two-by-fours. There's even a section of shelving to *hold* two-by-fours. "Rose keeps me organized."

We're returning to my yard with four studs each, and Whitey has already gotten my ladder out, which is leaning against the garage by the tree. We're telling Wilber that we sure do appreciate the generous donation of the lumber. I am relieved that he isn't causing a stink about defacing the neighborhood with a crummy tree house.

"You're going to need a level." Wilber says, as if he knows exactly what we're going to do.

"Yeah, as a matter of fact." I have no idea where mine is at the moment, since the last time I used it was to hang a big picture for Wendy.

"No problem. It's on shelf two, section three in the garage. Be back in a second with the level, two more studs and the skill saw. I'll get the extension cord, too."

"How long do you think it'll be before Rose finds him?"

"It'll be too soon, 'cause he don't wanna go home." Whitey is enjoying this.

◆   ◆   ◆

Its three o'clock, and we have installed two-by-fours on the two east offshoots of the tree, and the two west offshoots. They're level, thanks to Good Neighbor, Wilber. We started with one nail in the end of one eight-footer. We put the level on the top, and I nailed the other end into the next offshoot and cut off the excess, so it wouldn't stick out too far. I'm the ladder, hammer, and saw man. Wilber is the hand-up man and construction engineer. Whitey is sitting on an aluminum lawn chair with his foot propped up on another chair. He's drinking a tepid beer and shouting orders.

"Put another two nails in at each end, and we go to the other side." I oblige him.

The other side is tricky, because it has to be at the same height as the first. Wilber has a plan in his head. "We'll cut this next board off a little bit so we're not fumbling around with too much weight." I'm doing this, and I'm not great with a hand saw with my feet wedged in an awkward manner in the fork of the tree. "Now, pound a nail almost through the end of this one, and we'll just barely get it stuck to the tree. I'll lay a piece of wood on top of the two boards and put the level over that. When it reads level, we'll pound her in all the way. Same goes for the other end. It's too bad that trees don't grow symmetrical." Wilber has his own brand of humor. Miraculously, we have a front base and a back base. They're level, and the same height. We nailed the hell out of 'em. Now, we start doing the uprights. There is a nagging thought in my head about the original wood that is waiting in my garage. I'm hoping that the blue, glowing stuff has settled down. Wilber is bound to ask questions about that.

"Wil**BER**! We need to get going! Where are you? We told the Beckwiths we'd be there by four!"

"Over here, at Warren's house! Be right there, Honey Pot!" He looks like somebody took his ice cream cone away, and says he'll be back over to help later if we're still at it. You can almost bet we'll still be at it. Wilber is walking away looking dejected. "Buggars." He says, along with some other comments about hating bridge and the boring evening with the Beckwiths.

"Old Wilber will probably make sure it's the shortest bridge game anyone ever played. He'll be back. Where's your wheel barrow?" Whitey has had only one beer, so I'm hoping I can get a little help out of him, now that I've lost my best engineer.

"In the back of the garage."

"I'm on it." He says and pushes himself up from the folding chair and gallops toward the garage. It isn't long before Whitey and I have the wheel barrow piled to capacity. "There ya go, Buddy." I take it that I'm going to be doing the pushing and transporting. After a couple more loads the wood is all by the side of the garage where we need it. "Get on up there, Buddy. I'll hand the stuff up to you, since I didn't have very good luck in a tree on the last go 'round."

◆   ◆   ◆

It hasn't been going that well. It is six o'clock, and we've spent the last three hours figuring out the *access* to the darn thing. Would it be a platform? A closed in house? Would it have a roof? The Trooper isn't the most agile little guy with his double joints and a bit of awkwardness. He may be afraid of heights, so we are having to make everything as stable and unthreatening as possible. The most important feature of this house MUST be a western view of the sky. We're pushing on with these specifications in mind.

It is now nine thirty. Whitey and I are standing back from the tree, and each of us has a beer in hand. Whitey's fourth, my first. I'm tired as hell, but it has been worth it. We're strolling around the tree looking up at a forty-eight square foot platform, (8' by 6') for the imagination-challenged soul. There's a ladder going up the trunk of the tree. You climb up the ladder on the east side, and you go through an opening in the floor that's three by two. If Whitey or I gain any weight before the final caper, our asses are grass

After you've negotiated the opening, you slip a board over the hole, so you have your floor space back. You are in an enclosed room, except for the west side, which has a partial wall that is four feet high, and you can look out at the sky.

Uprights are supporting the walls, and there's a roof in case of rain. When you look out the open side, you are nine feet in the air and, hopefully, looking at Venus when the time is right.

"I'm damn proud of you!" Whitey says.

"Couldn't have done it without you and Wilber." I'm giving my pal a pat on the back just as Whitey's cell phone rings. It's Connie.

"We're fine. We got 'er DUN, do you believe it?"

Whitey chats for a couple of minutes with Connie, while I throw some extra end pieces of wood in the wheel barrow and take them to the garage. I'm starving and not looking forward to the game of chance, when I close my eyes to select my TV dinner for tonight.

"Connie wants you to come over for supper. Pot roast. She fixed it in case it needed to be put on hold if we went late." I'm rescued.

"I'm there. Lemme take a quick shower. You go on ahead. Tell Connie thanks, and I'll be there in about a half hour." I also tell my pal to be careful *driving*.

Whitey gallops a little slower to his truck, and I am praying he makes it home in one piece. I'm taking another look at our masterpiece. Two shining eyes are looking down at me from the roof of the tree house. "You get down here, Barnabus! Supper time!"

I just have to take time to climb that ladder. I'm like that little kid back in 1949. I manage to get myself up through the floor opening and put the cover over it. I'm looking westward, and there she is. Venus is low in the sky and on her way to the horizon. It all rushes back to me, and I can almost feel that brace on my leg and Whitey holding on to me. I can see the overwhelming wave of white, whirling mist taking over the house. I can see Whitey flinging my leg brace out the window and see it spin into nothing but a glowing orb and disappear. I can feel myself shivering from the trauma. I remember moving my legs left and right, and finally marching on this very floor with strong legs, and I'm singing and stomping along with the beat. I'm thinking of the Trooper and of Wendy. I'm still wondering if I'm doing the right thing.

I'm showered, dressed in some clean duds, and backing my car out of the driveway. I look up at the tree house, which is now glowing bright, blue and sending streamers to the ground like the Northern Lights. It has also taken on a bright, orange halo over the roof. I'm hesitating to leave the thing and wondering if there is any way I can cover it up. Whitey was wrong when he said it would mellow down after it was all put together. I'm afraid Wilber will be in for a surprise when he gets home. I'm telling myself that I'll deal with this later. Too hungry and too tired. I did remember to feed Barnabus.

A TREE HOUSE I SAW IN A YARD OUT IN FLORENCE
I'm more aware of tree houses, now.

25

A HEAP OF PEOPLE

I wheel into Whitey's driveway, and it is about ten o'clock. Whitey greets me at the door, and the house smells like roast beef. My mouth is watering now. The news is on the TV in the living room, and there are three TV trays set up. "Not gonna be formal tonight!" Connie yells from the kitchen. Whitey tells me to come on out and fill my plate, and they don't have to ask me twice. I'm carrying my plate full of beef, mashed potatoes and gravy, "church casserole". (Connie calls it that, but it is green beans and mushroom soup with pieces of bacon all mixed up together.) I have my second beer of the day in my left hand. Whitey's at least on his fifth. We're plunking our dinners down onto the trays, when the news anchor on TV catches our attention.

"Police say that they haven't found any explanation for this phenomenon, but the problem is the traffic. They have called in extra officers for traffic control, and we're told that the line of cars is about a mile long and moving slowly past a home in the university area. Neighbors are complaining that there are vehicles parked in their yards. They estimate around five hundred people on foot in the yards surrounding the property."

Connie, Whitey and I haven't taken a bite of our dinners, because we notice that the house that we can see behind the roving reporter is mine. The news person is shoving a microphone nearly into the mouth of a very large woman. "Well, we was drivin' home from gittin' a cheeseburger when Clyde, that's my husband, says "Lookit that!" And there it was. Looked like a big, puffy cloud that was all kinds of colors comin' out from the back of that house, right there, so we stopped and just watched and watched, and before long, there was hunnerts of cars comin' around and causin' this here traffic jam."

I'm looking at Whitey, and he says to me, "Might as well sit back and enjoy your dinner, Buddy Boy. Ain't nobody home at your house except the cat. Maybe it'll all clear out after while. By the way, did you remember to hang the board with the names on it inside the house?"

"No."

"Do it, before you go to bed. That's why you have your basic three-ring-circus, you know. The light show will stop when the plaque is hung. The house just isn't finished, and its complaining."

"Why didn't you tell me that *before* you left my house?"

"Forgot. I shouldn't have to tell you everything."

"Well, you seem to have every other damn rule up in that head of yours!" I suddenly realize that while I'm in my tirade, I'm sitting in front of a delicious supper cooked by Whitey's wife. I'm also realizing that if it weren't for Whitey, I would be a crip. "Sorry. It's been a long day ... a long week."

There's that big smile on Whitey's face, and his eyes are glowing in the flicker of the TV. "Eat, Buddy Boy."

"You need your strength, Warren." Connie sounds strangely like my mother.

I have managed to consume every bit of everything on my plate plus seconds and a piece of apple pie with ice cream on top. The goodbye's have been said and numerous thank you's on my part, since I'm still feeling guilty about my temper tantrum. Whitey says he'll give me a call in the morning, as I'm forcing my full stomach under the steering wheel of the Buick.

The drive home is about twenty minutes, and I'm rehearsing an explanation for the spectacle in my back yard. There isn't any answer that anybody will believe, so I just keep driving and hoping for the best. Two black and whites are at the curb, and only a few neighbors are hovering in the yard. Two of them are Wilber and Rose. I pull into my driveway and get out of my car, as the cops amble over to me, a man and a woman.

"Can you tell us what's going on in your back yard, Sir?"

I'm casually looking up at the billowing cloud, as if I've seen a million of them.

"That?"

Yessir." My mind is racing.

"Well, first of all, I'm sorry about all the trouble this seems to have caused."

"Just tell us what it is, Sir. Is it toxic?" Says the bad, male cop.

It's my cue. I'm on now, so I wade in. "Well, I've dabbled in chemistry all my life. I was always fascinated with it, and this project has more than gotten the results I planned on. And, by the way, it isn't toxic. But you see, I have always had an idea that through the use of chemistry, a guy could make things that are pleasing to a person's eye, like the stuff people put in their yards at Christmas ... lights. That kind of thing. I'm retired now, so I have time during the day to work on this stuff. So, this afternoon I put together a combination of things that I thought would put off a nice glow on something, and I decided that my grandson's tree house would be a perfect place to try it out. I painted the outside of it with this mixture, because I wanted to see what it would do at night. Well, it did it! More than I would ever imagine! I have stuff to neutralize it. Don't worry about that! It'll be gone before morning. I'll take care of it right away. Won't happen again, Officers."

Wilber is looking at me from a distance with his arms crossed just waiting to hear what I'll say next.

"What's your name, Sir?" Bad cop says.

"Warren Hearst, Sir."

"This is just a warning, Mr. Hearst. You caused quite a problem tonight. We'll do a drive-by tomorrow about dark and check things out, if you don't mind."

"Noooo Sir. Come right on ahead. It'll all be taken care of. You can bet on that."

The cops get in their two cars and are gone, but some of the neighbors can't help but give me a bunch of you-know-what, and they hang around until they get tired and go home to bed. It is now after midnight. Wilber is still here, waiting his turn.

"Now, I've heard everything. You know that? As one of the engineers on this project I think I'm entitled to an explanation. You said you weren't going to PAINT it!" I'm assuring Wilber that I will fill him in on the details, and he is going home at last.

It is after midnight, and no one is around that I can see. I'm in my sweat pants and black T-shirt with the Harley on the front. I have my flashlight, but I don't need it, because there's enough light coming in through the window from the glow of the tree house. I had stashed the plaque just inside the garage door and found it easily. Luckily, one of my hammers is on the peg board. I keep coffee cans full of nails of all sizes on a shelf. I had inherited these nails from my father when the folks had to move into assisted living.

This plaque project isn't planned very well. I'm trying to hold it under my left arm with the hammer in my left hand. I have about six large nails in my mouth. I'm using my right hand to pull myself up the ladder. The flashlight is stuck in my waist band. I manage to pull myself up through the floor entrance and let the nails, hammer and the piece of wood with the names on it fall to the floor. Suddenly, something claws its way up the tree trunk. I hear a muffled howl, as Barnabus streaks between my legs and winds up sitting there in a rainbow of colors with a mouse in his mouth. I find myself with a flashlight down in my pants … lit. I don't need the darn thing in all these whirling lights, but I'm hoping I *will* need it after the plaque is up and it suddenly gets dark.

I'm choosing the wall on the right for the plaque. It's not a Better Homes decision. I bang two nails in each end of the board. Good enough. I'm staying here, hoping things will die down and watching Barnabus play with his catch. I hate that stuff, but nature is nature. There isn't any Venus out there now, but I have my palms on the ledge of the west open wall, just waiting for all this damn light to go away.

"I knew you'd be up here."

I have just bitten my tongue, because I jumped at the sound of Wilber's voice behind me and hit my head on the ceiling.

"Criminey, Wilber! Couldn't you have *warned* me you were coming up here?" Something wet is now running down my forehead. Musta hit my head pretty good. Another project, another injury. That's me. No free lunch. Goes clear back to childhood.

"I'm your co-engineer! I have an investment in the project and a right to see it through!"

I'm too tired to go into a long explanation about how I decided to build this thing. I would have to lie to him about the real reason, and I'm too tired to think up another long, tall tale like the one I told the cops. Wilber is just beginning to query me about this glowing mass, when suddenly we're standing here in the dark.

"Go to bed, Wilber. We're both pooped. I'll talk to you tomorrow, and I do thank you for all your help, neighbor. Watch your step going back down the ladder. I'll hold the flashlight so you can see."

It is after one. Wilber is probably in bed now, and so am I. I don't think I'll have too much trouble getting to sleep, but first I have to deal with Barnabus, who has suddenly jumped into my bed with his dead mouse in his mouth. I'm getting back up to flush the toilet for its burial at sea.

26

THE TROOP COMES HOME

I'm not up yet. I'm looking over at my large number digital clock, and it says ten thirty. Even Barnabus is still curled up next to my head, and I'm making sure I don't get in the line of fire of his breath after last night's kill. I'm surprised that I haven't heard from Wendy. I don't expect any neighbors to bother me yet, since they were all up half the night, just like I was. As I'm pushing the sheet off my body, Barnabus leaps off the bed and is sitting by his bowl in roughly three seconds. We take care of cat meals first and foremost at my house, since nothing else can get done until the cat has been served.

A shower is sounding good and necessary, so I'm shuffling toward the bathroom when the phone rings. I'm thinking it's probably Wendy. *Or the cops or Whitey or Wilber or the Media.* "You OK Daddy?" I'm figuring that she is wondering why I haven't shown up at the hospital yet, but she won't say that to me.

"Hi, Sweetheart. I'm on my way in just a little bit. Running late this morning, because Whitey's project went later than we thought, and Connie made me stay for dinner. One thing lead to another, and I got to bed late. I couldn't believe how late I slept this morning!" I'm getting good at fuzzy little white lies.

"I *saw* the news last night, Daddy. You told me you were *stacking wood* with Whitey! What the hell are you up to? What was that about a tree house?"

I'm busted. Here I go again, making things up to cover my you-know-what. I wind up telling Wendy about the tree house without going into great detail. She doesn't know anything about the one in 1949. She only knows that I miraculously got well from having polio when I was a child. "It's supposed to be a surprise for the Trooper, Sweetheart. He's going to love it, and I can't wait for him to come see it. It's real special. How's Trooper doing?" I'm hoping this question diverts her from the subject of the tree house and the coverage on the news, and I'm squeezing my eyes shut and bracing myself for what comes next.

"Yeah, I saw some of that *special stuff* on TV Dad, and I'm not quite satisfied with that sketchy, understated explanation! BUT, to answer your question, it's good news! The Kid is coming home this afternoon. He'll have to take it easy, take some more medications and see the doc in a few days. You don't have to bother coming up to the hospital, Daddy. We'll be home in a couple of hours, and I'll call you when we get there. Don't worry."

Wendy isn't mad at me. I know her. She's just giving me a hard time. I'm sure she was having fun making me squirm over the phone, and I'll get the old third degree when I see her. All in fun. I'm going up there as soon as I can get there. No way would I sit here at the house waiting for her to call, while Trooper is still in the hospital. Not in my nature. "You can't get rid of me that easy, Sweetheart. I'll be dressed and up there shortly with some rolls and coffee."

As we're saying goodbye, Wendy does sound happy that I'm coming. Good decision on my part. I'm punching in Whitey's phone number to update him on the rest of the story.

"You survived."

"Barely. I'm not in jail."

"Cops, huh?"

"Yep. Several, if you count the ones on traffic control."

"You tell 'em a good story?"

"Good enough. Don't ask."

"You put the names up in the tree house?"

"Yep."

"It worked?"

"Yep."

"You OK?"

"Cut my damn head."

"What's new? You talk to Wendy?"

"Yep. Trooper is coming home this afternoon. He's much better. I'm having breakfast up there in a few minutes after I pick up some rolls. I'll give you a call tonight, and thank Connie again for the late supper. And you too, Pal. For everything."

"No problem, Buddy. Let's watch the weather reports and shoot for Saturday, that's *tomorrow*! Trooper needs to climb that ladder! Whattya think?"

"Wendy's gonna ixnay that idea. Too damn soon. The Kid was pretty sick, you know."

"Maybe, maybe not. You soften her up today, and I'll call her later. I think there's a chance she'll buy into it, somehow."

"Yeah, when pigs fly. But you've pulled off harder things than that before, so …"

"Yep." Click.

◆   ◆   ◆

I'm on the elevator with some of those cream-filled things with chocolate frosting, when the door opens, just in time for me to see the lunch cart coming down the hall. When I start the day running late, the whole day is screwed up. The pastry will get eaten, I'm sure. Probably by me. I'm greeted loudly as I enter Trooper's room. "HI, PAW PAW! I WENT FOR A WALK WITH JULIE, AND MAMA CAME TOO. I'M HAVING A WEENIE AND TATO CHIPS AND CHOCOLATE MILK AND JELLO. YOU AND MAMA GO HAVE LUNCH NOW!"

"Hi, Daddy! Sounds like our lunch time is already planned for us."

I give Trooper a kiss and tell him I'll see him later, and off we go to the cafeteria. I'm stopping at the nurses' station to give them the pastry for the break room. I know that's one way to make food disappear.

We're sitting at a large table, way back in the corner of the cafeteria by a sunny window. Wendy's having a chef salad, and I'm having beef tips on noodles. I should have scanned the whole selection of food before I made my choice. I just grabbed the first thing that I thought looked palatable. This stuff can be compared to library paste and dog food.

"Sooooooo, DAD! Tell me the story about last night! I guess I can't let you and Whitey out of my sight, can I?"

"You caught me, all right! Looks like I can't keep a secret worth a poop, but you'll go crazy when you see it, Sweetheart! It's great! Perfect for a kid. Trooper and I can have some real laughs up there when the weather gets warmer. It'll be our special hiding place. We can take stuff up there to play with, and I'll read to him and show him how to BEAMSHOOT ... all that good stuff!"

"BEAMSHOOT?"

"I'll have to tell you that story sometime. Anyway, Sweetheart, I'm real anxious to show it to the Trooper. Hope I made it roomy enough for us two big guys. Every kid has to experience a tree house. Nothin' like that nowadays ... just those stupid, squeaky-clean, square boxes on redwood stands in peoples' back yards with swings and plastic slides and green tents over the tops. Too *planned!* They're just like everybody else's, all squatty on the ground next to sandboxes that probably are filled with cat poop. This is a *real* tree house with ladder steps up the trunk and a *trap door* in the floor, and its *members only!* You build it as you go and hope for the best. "

Wendy is crunching real slow on her lettuce and chicken and staring at me as if I had forgotten to take my meds.

"Daddy … How's he going to get up there? You know how uncoordinated Bernie Bern is. I don't want him to get hurt. What if he … *falls?*" I know she doesn't want to hurt my feelings.

"I'll make sure he's safe, honey. It's worth it, mostly to me, right now. This special present has been in the planning stages for a long time, and now is the perfect time. If it weren't for old Whitey, we wouldn't have the tree house to begin with. He'll be hurt if the Trooper doesn't have this opportunity to see the kind of thing us guys used to do when we were kids."

"There's plenty of time, Dad. Bernie Bern is always going to be a child."

"OK, Sweetheart, we'll make it happen when you say so." *I want him to see it before he gets sicker.*

"What were all those people looking at on the news last night?" Wendy is derailing me on this issue of Trooper's visit.

"I was just doing some rather theatrical experiments on the tree house … some signal lights and such. A guy has to have *signals* he can send when he's in his tree house! Would your old dad do anything that would be dangerous for a kid? 'Course not! All those onlookers were just gawking."

I am so full of bullshit, I can hardly stand myself nowadays. I feel I have sent Wendy on a colossal guilt trip now, making her think she'll disappoint me by keeping me from my life dream. It's really not fair, but I'm doing it anyway. I've gotten used to taking risks just by knowing Whitey all these years, and I'm hoping I don't lose the love of my daughter after all is said and done. It's a risk I can hardly bear to think about, but I just have to go forward with this. I just have to, and that's all there is to it. If I don't …

We're on our way back to Trooper's room, and it's quiet in the elevator. "I love you, Daddy." Wendy whispers. That's all I need for now.

It's two PM, and the three of us are riding down to the lobby with a red HUSKERS backpack, a BOO BOO bear and prescriptions to be filled. Wendy loads Trooper into her car and straps him into the passenger seat. I toss his stuff into the back. They're heading home, and I'm picking up the meds in my car to take to Wendy's house. One less thing for her to do. I'm offering to bring them supper. "We're having BREAKFAST for supper, Daddy! Scrambled eggs and toast with jelly. Bernie Bern loves that. Want to stay and eat with us?"

"Thanks, Honey, but I have a mess of paper work to get done for Kiwanis, and I have to call a bunch of guys for the golf outing." More bull coming out of my mouth.

Everyone is kissing everyone, and I'm now heading home, hoping I have made some headway toward getting Trooper to his new tree house.

I'm feeding Barnabus a snack before I give Whitey a call. The cat just looks at me like I'm nuts. Five little Fishy Treats are in front of him on the kitchen floor. On examination of the packet, I discover that they're the *soft* ones, not the tartar control kind that are crunchy. Barnabus won't even touch them. I open a can of tuna as an apology and punch in Whitey's number. I know. I'm pathetic.

27

FAST TALK AND PRESENTS

I think Whitey bends the rules just a bit when it comes to his powers of persuasion. He's a natural when it comes to convincing a person about something, but the line is so fine that a guy doesn't always know whether it's the *gift*, or just perseverance and determination on his part. But, I know that he knows the rules. I'm telling you this, because it has to do with the outcome of our efforts to bring the Trooper to his new tree house.

I've seen Wendy and Trooper everyday this week. Wendy has taken these days off from work. She's lucky to have the job she has, because they understand her special circumstances and are flexible to her needs with her son. It's my guess that she believes Trooper will be able to go back to his special school next week. However …

It's Friday, and I'm at her front door with sandwiches from Subway. I can hear the floor thumping as the Trooper hurries to let me in. "HI, PAW PAW! COME SEE THE EFLUNTS AND JAFFERS!" He's watching the Discovery Channel. "EFLUNTS GOT LONG NOSES, AND JAFFERS GOT LONG NECKS! IF THEY FIGHT, IT GONNA BE FUNNY!"

Wendy comes out of the bathroom just as I'm giving Trooper a big hug and smashing all the sandwiches between us.

"You're spoiling us rotten, Daddy."

"My favorite pastime! How's everybody today?" I'm trying to lay the groundwork for my invitation to the Trooper for an over night stay *tomorrow*. Trooper has stayed with me many times, so this isn't an unusual thing for me to invite him. He loves to come, and I always try to think of something special for us to do. Most times, it's popcorn and a rented movie.

"He's much, much better, Daddy. In fact, I'm trying to keep the lid on too much activity too soon. He keeps wanting to go outside for a walk and go to the park, but I don't think he should yet."

Wendy is wearing her hair down today. It's long and beautiful with a bit of wave to it like her mother had. Wendy wears it up in a knot most of the time when she's at work for a more professional look. Today she looks like her honey-blonde mother.

I'm looking at my grandson and thinking of all the things he could be doing and the friends he could have and all the millions of things he could know about and see. He's twelve. There should be baseball gloves hanging on handle bars of bikes, music, funny jokes, trying out cuss words with his pals behind his mother's back, **kate** boards, learner's permits, cars, college, girls, a career, a wife, children. I should back up a little ... puberty.

I'm taking a huge leap to the subject of the tree house. "I don't suppose you've given any thought about when Trooper can see his *you-know-what* ... "

"Oh, didn't I TELL you? I had just the *nicest* talk with Whitey last night! He stopped by! Brought me the prettiest bouquet of fresh flowers (they're out on the kitchen table) and two candy bars for Bernie Bern, his favorite ... Snickers bars! Wasn't that sweet of him? Connie came too! They were here quite a while, and Whitey got on the subject of tree houses and how he loved his as a kid and how you and he used to spend hours and hours there. He said it was the best thing ever to happen in his childhood. He really went nostalgic on me, Daddy, talking and talking about that old tree house and the good times you guys had then. He said it saved his life, but he didn't go into that. He told me to ask you about BEAMSHOOTING sometime! You HAVE to tell me that story! But, I guess you're going to tell Bernie Bern first tomorrow night when he gets to go up in his new tree house! I'll bring him over at supper time so you can do the TV dinner thing with him. He loves that. Don't you, Kiddo?"

"YEP. I CAN PET BARNAPUSS AND CLOSE MY EYES AND GET A SURPRISE SUPPER OUT OF THE FREEZER!"

Whitey's done it again.

28

OVERDUE SPECULATIONS ON THE FUTURE

It's about four thirty, and I'm sitting here in my recliner with a stiff Jack Daniels in my hand. I've called Whitey, and it's all set. I asked him if he had used *unfair* tactics to persuade Wendy to let the Trooper come tomorrow night. He said no. Said he was so passionate about it, he didn't need *unfair* tactics. All I know is that I didn't get the job done myself. I tried, but I was too timid and much too close to my daughter to risk making her mad and question my sanity. Trooper is supposed to get here at five. Whitey will be here around eight. We'll all have ice cream and Oreo cookies, which I picked up at the store today. I don't want anything to seem rushed tomorrow night. It wouldn't be good to scare Trooper. Even though he is challenged mentally, he has a little antenna that tells him when people are nervous, and I will be nervous. I'll try not to show it, but I'm sure Whitey will be entertaining enough to cover my anxiety. I wonder if my grandson will want me to call him "Trooper" after tomorrow.

Plan ahead. A wonderful piece of advice, I've always thought. How can I possibly know what's ahead? I just know that GOOD is ahead, even though there will be the most unimaginable trauma of biblical proportions to go through on the other side of this ... for everyone who has ever known Wendy and Trooper.

The first thought that hit me when I finally decided to do this thing, was what would Wendy's little guy look like? Then my thoughts went from one thing to another like links in a chain. How does a guy talk to someone who has turned into someone else with a mental capacity that has undergone a huge change? What will Trooper do with these new possibilities at first? Will he even talk at all? Will he never stop talking? How will the educators handle this? How long will it take for Trooper to reach is own new level? I'm in such a state right now, that I can hardly face the possibilities that are ahead for Trooper and his mother. And then there's the *media*. I think about Trooper's health, and all of the other facets of this become trivial. I'm doing the only thing that seems right and good. I'm having another Jack Daniels. I'm not hungry. I'm bracing for the tsunami.

There is another aspect about this tree house thing that has been in my mind, but kind of buried deep down, so that it won't drive me crazy. It makes me scared as hell, because it is a reminder of the emotions my own mother and father and sister went through at the sight of me without my crutch and leg brace, as I danced around our dining room table and mounted the stairs to my attic, two at a time, and finally asked if I could get my bike out of the garage. But I was always *me*. I was *me* even afterward. The great question is this: *Will there not be even a whisper of Trooper left? Will I have taken all reminders of Wendy's beloved son away from her?*

I have to keep reminding myself of Whitey's words. He had said that part of the gift is that no one who loves that *chosen* person will be mad because of any change. It's hard for me to assume that, but it's the only thing that keeps me brave. There will be a lot of crap to go through before things settle down. No more to drink for me.

29

WHERE THREE HAVE GATHERED

It is seven o'clock, and I have had a reasonably good night's sleep. I'm spending the day contemplating Trooper's arrival. There's a reasonable mix of TV dinners in the freezer, but I'm making sure that when the little guy closes his eyes and reaches for his surprise supper, he WILL select spaghetti and meat balls. The top four dinners are all alike, and the rest are much less interesting. I have the chocolate chip-chocolate ice cream and the Oreos for dessert tonight with Whitey. That'll wire us up good. I have donuts and OJ for breakfast. What's a grandpa for? I'm wondering if Trooper will even be here at breakfast time.

Barnabus has left me a present on the steps of the back porch, since he was out all night. There are two legs, part of a tail, an eye and some innards with pieces of black fur on them. I'm sweeping this disgusting remainder of a vole on to the want ad section of the paper. Its wrapped securely and twisted at the top. Of course, the trash collectors won't be here for several days. It's a rule. I'm also climbing up into the tree house to make sure there's nothing resembling this up there. I pull myself up through the trap door, and it's a lot harder than when I was a young buck. I see the names on the board that I nailed to the wall. It's probably my mind playing games with me, but I think I hear a low hum like an old radio that is on with the tubes glowing inside but not on any station. I'm putting my ear close to the names, and I'm glad no one can see me. There's an energy, and the wood feels warm on the side of my face. I don't plan on climbing up here again until tonight, even though I'll be tempted as hell.

I notice a few cars are going slow in front of my house. People are still rubbernecking the property, hoping to see something in the daylight. I just wave at them and smile. I'm stepping up my pace to get in the side door before any of the neighbors, namely Wilber, catch me. I'm not in any mood for questions.

The coffee is done, and I'm having a frozen waffle, toasted with blue berries, banana, and syrup on top. The TV is on, and the local weather girl is predicting a clear night. A lot can happen in a short time in Nebraska when it comes to the weather, but I'm not going to spend the whole day dwelling on what the sky might do.

I'm keeping myself busy and trying not to rehearse what might happen tonight. I'm washing the sheets and putting them back on my bed right out of the dryer. Barnabus is helping me, of course, which makes that job take a little longer. I'm afraid to call Wendy. What if I call and she says the Trooper doesn't feel good? *Stop that*. She answers on the second ring. "Hi, Daddy!"

"How's my kid?"

"Oh, Daddy, he's so excited about tonight! This day is going by soooo slowly for him. He keeps asking if it's time to go to Paw Paw's house. I swear, I'm going to have to give in and take him to the park for a little bit to make the time pass for us both!"

"Don't let him get hurt."

"I won't, Dad."

"He's coming at five? You sure you don't want me to come get him?"

"No, Dad. I'll bring him. I'm going out for dinner with a couple of gals from the office tonight. RUDE COMPANY is playing downtown at the WATER-FRONT, and we'll probably stay for a couple of sets. I won't be too late, and I'll have my cell on if you need me."

"OK, Honey. Tell the Trooper that Paw Paw's all ready for him!"

A band at the pub. Good. I wouldn't want Wendy to be living like a nun, and I don't blame her for wanting to do something different when she gets the chance. This just fortifies the decision Whitey and I made for the Trooper. Lives are going to be changed. Everybody involved is going to be doing different things shortly, if all goes as planned.

◆   ◆   ◆

It's finally four o'clock, and I don't know what I've done all day, except wash sheets, dispose of a dead vole carcass, and go to Subway for a sandwich.

My cell phone rings ... Whitey. I'm happy, because this kind of confirms that we will all converge tonight, for sure.

"The Kid's comin' in about an hour, right?"

"Yep. Havin' TV dinners. You're coming at about eight?"

"Make it seven thirty. Connie's drivin' me nuts asking me questions. She says it sounds creepy that I'm going to spend the evening with you and Trooper. Not that you're creepy, but it's not even Trooper's birthday! She got real sarcastic and asked me if you had decided you were gay. But she was laughin' when she said it."

"It kind of IS his birthday, if you think about it."

"Yep. It kind of is. Make sure you have a pair of sweat pants and a sweat shirt for the Kid." Click

I'm not commenting on Connie's humor, and I honestly hadn't thought about some different duds for Trooper. It kind of raises the hair on the back of my neck when I think about it. I've caught myself playing the game of *WHAT IF* all day, and all of those scenarios seem to be negative when they don't necessarily have to be. I'm a number ten worrier on that scale of one to ten.

I'm digging out a pair of stretchy, gray sweat pants and a T-shirt from a drawer in the bedroom, when the door bell rings. Too early for the Trooper, so I'm worrying that it might be the police doing a follow-up on the circus that took place here recently. It's Whitey. I'm taken off guard, but I'm a little bit relieved, because Whitey has a way of making a guy forget his worries. With the sweats over my arm, I open the door. There's a huge smile on his face, like a kid that can't wait to go to the circus.

"I came early. Couldn't stand Connie following me around askin' questions. I thought maybe you could use some support. How many TV dinners you got?"

"About sixty two and I'm glad you came early. I was fidgeting around here, driving myself nuts. Trooper is due here soon. Want a beer?" It seems to me that Whitey is healing damn fast for a guy his age. He is wearing only an Ace bandage on his ankle, now.

"A beer sounds good. I see you got the Kid some sweats. Those are good. Nice and flexible for whatever happens. He'll have to put 'em on beforehand. We'll tell him they're for climbing trees … the special uniform for the new members of the TREE HOUSE CLUB."

We have about half an hour before Trooper comes. We're at the kitchen table, and the conversation turns to the plan to get the kid into the tree house safely.

"I think we ought to do what we did for you back in '49. I'll climb up first. You'll be behind him for support. I'll already be up there to grab his hands, and we'll just swoop him on up through the trap door."

"Sounds like a plan, but you gotta remember he's heavier than you might think. He's not very tall, but there's a lot of flesh around his frame. How is your ankle?" Whitey ignores this last question.

"You nervous? You act nervous, Pal. I can understand that."

"Not as much now as I was earlier. I'm glad Connie drove you out of the house."

"You've survived lots of capers with me, and you're still here, all in one piece. You'll make it, *Warren*."

"Hey, Pal, if I remember right, there were a few mishaps along the way when I almost *didn't* survive."

The front door bursts open and thundering feet run to the kitchen. "I'M HERE, PAW PAW. YOU HAVING BEER? I WANT SOME BEER, TOO!" Trooper gives me a huge hug and a kiss on the cheek.

"I couldn't keep him home a second longer, Dad. Hi, Whitey! Good to see you!" Wendy is obviously ready to go out tonight. No corporate clothes. She looks different. I don't know whether I'm happy about how she looks. Her blonde hair is down to her shoulders, and she has great big, loopy earrings on. She's wearing tight jeans and a leather jacket. I just don't know.

"Don't worry about us, Sweetheart. We have a fun bachelor party planned tonight … just us guys. Right, Trooper?" I'm noticing that Whitey's pink eyes are riveted on Wendy. The old fart.

Trooper has found Barnabus and is chasing him into the bedroom, but Barnabus always finds a place where he is unreachable.

"Gotta go, Dad! Good to see you, Whitey! I didn't know you were coming! Thanks again for the flowers! Bye bye, Bernie Bern!" She shouts toward the bedroom, but Trooper is busy looking for Barnabus and doesn't say anything.

"Bye, Honey. Have a good time." *But not too good.* I give her a peck on the cheek and tell her I'll see her tomorrow. *Or sooner.*

Whitey is wearing a big grin, and those pink eyes of his are following Wendy's rear as she sachets to the front door. He looks at me with the same grin after the front door is shut.

"Don't say it, Pal."

Trooper comes back into the kitchen. His lower lip is protruding, and he looks like he might cry. "WHERE'S BARNAPUSS? I CAN'T FIND HIM. HE'S HIDING FROM ME. HE DOESN'T LIKE ME."

I tell Trooper that kitties do that sometimes. "They like to play hide and seek. He'll come out in a little while for his supper." That seems to do the trick. "Sit down at the table, and I'll get you a glass of pop."

"JULIE SAYS IT'S SODA!"

"OK, it's soda. You know best!"

"THAT'S WHAT JULIE SAID AT THE HOPSICLE."

Whitey's holding his empty beer can over his head, and I take the cue to get out two more beers.

We're doing the small talk thing at the kitchen table, and it's now about six o'clock. I turn on the local news. "... doppler radar shows a severe storm system out around York, but we're not expecting anything here in our area until around ten o'clock tonight. It's a slow-moving system. Stay tuned to channel six, and we'll have continual updates throughout the evening. And now, here's Dave with the sports."

"We better stay on schedule, Buddy boy, and hope that Venus isn't behind the clouds at nine. I'm thinking we'll get up there by eight thirty to catch her the second she shows herself. I've kept track of her for quite a while, and it's about nine when she shows up right now. I'm a StarDate Magazine buff, and I keep close tabs on her."

"I HUNGRY."

"Shall we tell your Paw Paw to get goin' on our supper?"

"YEAH, SUPPER, SUPPER, SUPPER!" Trooper is bouncing on the kitchen chair.

I'm dazzling Whitey with my red, paper placemats. While the other two guys sit drinking, I'm putting forks, spoons and paper napkins on the table. The topper is my presentation of the raspberry-marshmallow jello salad for the Trooper and potato salad for Whitey and me, all bought at the deli. We're making a big deal of the selection of the dinners. Trooper gets to go first, so he can eat while Whitey and I wait for our gourmet trays.

"SKETTY!"

"Hold your horses. It's coming right up!" I slip Trooper's dinner into the zapper, while Whitey inspects the array of boxes. He winds up with Swiss Steak, and I tell him, "Just get one out for me, any kind." It turns out to be Flakey Breaded Halibut. I forgot that was in there. I'm putting bowls on the table for the salad, when I notice that Trooper has managed to put his raspberry jello on top of his green beans. I don't really blame him. The table talk ranges from favorite food to Special Olympics, to the weather, to Trooper's school, and to tree houses. All subjects are ones where we can include the little guy in the conversation. Whitey's pink eyes keep looking up at my wall clock. It's now seven. I'm feeling like I'm in one of those dreams where I can't run fast enough. I turn the TV back on to the weather channel.

"Turn the damn thing off, Pal. It ain't gonna do us any good. We can listen to those guys until the cows come home, but it is what *it is*. Let's have that ice cream. Right, Trooper?"

"YEAH, PAW PAW! CHOCOLATE! AND **COOKIES!**"

Whitey's right, but I'm on number ten and about ready to leap up to twelve or thirteen on my worry scale. Apprehension doesn't even come close to how I'm feeling.

What if it doesn't work?

I ask Whitey to throw the empty plastic trays in the trash. I'm wiping up the trail of jello from the salad bowl to where Trooper's beans used to be.

The ice cream and cookies disappear in less than five minutes, and we are coming to the time for putting on special uniforms for new Tree House Club members. Trooper has dribbled raspberry jello and chocolate ice cream down the front of his yellow sweat shirt and jeans, so Whitey uses this as an opener for changing clothes. "I bet that wet stuff feels icky on your skin, doesn't it, Little Guy?"

"No." Trooper is just staring at him with his fat, little tongue lying on his lower lip. Whitey's eyes are a more intense pink, I'm noticing.

"Yes, it does. It feels REAL icky. I would hate that, wouldn't you? BLAH!" Whitey is doing his *thing*. Trooper just looks down at his belly.

"YEAH, BLAH! REAL ICKY. I DON'T LIKE ICKY. BLAH, BLAH, BLAH."

"Wanna put on your special stuff for new Tree House Club members?"

"UH UH! WHAT'S A TREE HOUSE?"

"Well, Little Buddy, there's one in the back yard. Waaay up in Paw Paw's tree by the garage! It's YOURS! And you're gonna be a MEMBER, probably even the *PRESIDENT*, which means you gotta wear the UNIFORM!" Whitey is real convincing.

Whitey gives me the "go ahead" look, and I grab the gray sweats and white T-shirt off the chair in the living room. "Take your shoes off, Trooper." He gives me a wary look. I have a pair of larger Nikes for him. They'll be too roomy now, but his feet might change in the end. They could be larger. Makes me shiver.

Whitey pops the T-shirt over my grandson's head. "Arms." Whitey helps get Trooper's square, little hands through the sleeves. Trooper pulls the shirt down over his belly. It's hanging down past his butt, and the sleeves droop below his elbows.

"TOO BIG. I WANT MY YELLOW SWEAT SHIRT. MAMA WANTS ME TO WEAR MY YELLOW SWEAT SHIRT!"

Whitey comes to the rescue. "Your mama wants you to be a REAL member of the Tree House Club. That means that you have to have the UNIFORM on, see? That'll make your mama real happy! We'll put your yellow one on AFTER you're a MEMBER! OK, Buddy? Now, let's get these SPECIAL club member pants on!" He is now decked out in my gray sweat pants that are ballooning at the bottoms, but Whitey moves right along and has the Nikes on Trooper's feet in a matter of seconds. "Lookit YOU! You look like a real member ALREADY, doesn't he Paw Paw?"

I'm having a little trouble keeping a straight face at the sight of Trooper with all those strange, big clothes hanging down on his short, stocky body. Trooper doesn't look convinced. He's not tuned into being cool or in style, but he is aware that these duds suck.

"WHERE'S BOO BOO BEAR?" I can see that his little antenna is out and that word "apprehensive" fits my grandson. I think he gets his fear from how I'm acting. The cords in my neck may be sticking out, and the adrenaline is kicking in. I'm worrying that my grandson might throw a big fit. Luckily, Wendy brought Boo Boo Bear along with Trooper's PJ's, and I'm rushing into the bedroom to get him. By the time I'm back, Whitey is on the job again.

"Whattya say we take Boo Boo up in that tree house, and he'll be a member, too? OK Guy? Yeah! There's Paw Paw with Boo Boo right now!" Whitey grabs the bear out of my hand. "You wanna be a Tree House Club Member too, don't ya, Boo Boo!" Whitey holds Boo Boo's face up to his ear. "He says yes!" Whitey is making the bear's head nod up and down. Trooper has a tiny smile on his face, and his tongue is sticking out further now. His eyes seem to be shining, maybe from tears that didn't quite make it out over the edge earlier.

"I GONNA TAKE BOO BOO UP THE TREE WITH ME!"

This whole process has now brought us up to eight fifteen.

"Let's head out there." Whitey is giving me an encouraging look, and Trooper isn't crying. One small step. The sun has gone down over the horizon, but it's still too light for Venus to show up. The sky is dark blue with brilliant pink in the west. There are a few black clouds showing up in the southwest, and I'm hoping they don't rush forward along the I-80 and wind up in a tornado in my back yard at precisely nine o'clock. *Stop that.*

Barnabus is sitting in the back kitchen window. I'm glad he's in, because I don't want him to get all tangled up in this process. The three of us are tromping through the wet grass toward the tree house that is holding so many memories and hope and anticipation for me.

"Lookit up there, Trooper! Isn't that cool?" I'm trying to be extra positive, because the little guy is kind of dragging his feet.

"See that ladder, Buddy? We're gonna go UP that ladder into our secret club house, just for guys! Watch me! I'll go up first and be right there to pull you up!"

"NO. I NOT GOIN' UP THERE. I GONNA FALL. MAMA SAYS I DON'T GO UP ON HIGH STUFF. I NOT A BAD BOY. MAMA SAYS I A GOOD BOY! I DO WHAT MAMA SAYS!"

Here is the very reason why Mr. Whitey Swift is invited to this party.

"Hey, Pal. Do you know what your mama told me today?" Whitey is kicking in with the bullshit, but that bullshit once saved his life as a kid. Right on the railroad tracks and Whitey just keeps cranking it out to this day.

"She told me that she always wanted you to be a member of the TREE HOUSE CLUB! She told me that if your Paw Paw ever made you a tree house, she would be so happy about that, 'cause then you could be a member of the TREE HOUSE CLUB! You would be real cool, and you would wear this UNI-FORM! And, guess what! When she comes to pick you up tomorrow, you can TELL her that you ARE a member of the TREE HOUSE CLUB, just like Paw Paw and your good friend, Whitey! How 'bout that, Trooper?"

"OK. YOU TAKE BOO BOO UP FIRST." Trooper is a very brave little guy, I'm thinking, and the knot in my stomach is now looser than it was a minute ago. *God, don't let him fall.*

There are eight steps to the top. I have put window handles at each end of each piece of wood that makes up the ladder. Whitey is already up there, lying on his stomach with his head sticking out and his arms reaching down toward the kid through the open trap door. He had no problem climbing the ladder with his gimpy ankle. "See, Buddy? I'm right here to grab you! You're gonna be fine." I can see that if the Trooper can get up the first three or four steps, he'll be within reach of Whitey. With Whitey's firm grasp on Trooper's hands and my palms on his butt, it's up, up, up, whether he wants to be or not.

I'm nervous. "Here we go, Trooper! You and me! Reach up and grab those handles, right there by your nose and put your foot on the first step, right there by your knee!" I guide his little hands to each handle, and I'm pointing to the step. His foot slips off the first time, but on the second try, he is about one foot off the ground. "Good boy! You're a real sport! Here we go again!" The second step is easier, and his hands have found the next two handles without my telling him. "One, two, and now THREE!" He starts to look down at me. "Don't look at Paw Paw, Little Guy. Just keep looking at Whitey ... see how funny he looks?"

"I SCARED, PAW PAW."

"Hey, Pal. Look up at me! Grab the next handle! You're doin' fine!" When Trooper starts to grasp the next handle, Whitey latches onto one little wrist, and then another. The Trooper is gasping for air and making little, high-pitched noises in his panic. My hands are now on his butt. "Push, Pal! We gonna land this fish!" And we do. Trooper is catapulted straight up through the trap door, swung around, and is safely away from the hole in the floor. I'm there in a few seconds. I'm shaking, and I can't imagine how my grandson did it. Bravery and a guardian angel at the top, I guess. I'm quickly placing the cover over the hole in the floor, and the house is holding three good-sized people and a Boo Boo bear.

"Whattya think, Buddy?" Whitey's arms are out, and his palms are up like a real estate agent presenting somebody a new house.

"I WANT BOO BOO." Trooper says. Comfort. Security, when there doesn't seem to be any. I'm thinking I would appreciate something to hold on to right now.

"Let's bring Boo Boo over here so he can see the sunset." I take Trooper's hand that isn't the one holding the bear by the ear. He's afraid to look over the half-wall we built for spying. It seems very high, now that I think about it. Whitey is standing on the other side of Trooper. The three of us are in a row, and it boggles my mind, when I think of what we all have in common. Such great needs we all have had, and one still has them.

The sky is a much darker blue now, and the pink at the horizon is almost gone. It's not quite dark yet ... still too much light. It's about ten minutes before nine, when Whitey takes a long look at me. He's sending me a message that it won't be long now. There comes that smile of his again. The one that says "It's gonna be OK, Pal. Stick with me." Trooper is holding his Boo Boo Bear and looking out at the sky. It's quiet, except for a few leaves rustling in the tree with the slight breeze that is coming up. The clouds are closer now.

"LOOKA UP THERE! WHAT'S THAT?"

Whitey and I answer, almost simultaneously, "Venus."

"She's a planet that looks down at you." I tell him. My knees are weak, and I can feel Whitey's hand touch my shoulder.

I can hear that hum again. The ledge of the half-wall is warm, even in the cool air. The floor is slightly vibrating, and we are buzzing, too. Trooper looks up at me. "Paw Paw." He puts his arms around my middle. He has dropped his bear. "Paw Paw!" He's breathing rapidly now, as I am. Whitey's eyes are radiating pink, and we're all bathed in it.

"We gotta both hold on to him for dear life, Pal. We gotta be locked ... here we go." The humming is making us deaf, it's so loud. We're braced, and now the blue fog is swirling around us. Venus is sending hot beams of red, yellow and orange in through the half-wall. The hum has turned into a great roar, like a giant train that's sailing out of the sky toward us. The wind has come up. It's furiously shaking the tree, and I'm afraid we all might go tumbling to the ground, if the nails I pounded in so industriously come lose. I know I can never forgive myself if that happens. **Think, Pal. Think real hard about the little guy! Think your greatest wishes for him, hold him and look at Venus.** It is hard to hear Whitey over the roar. My ears hurt real bad. Trooper is crying and shaking from fear, and I can feel him shuddering. The whirling, blue fog is so intense that it is taking our breath away. **I never saw anything like this! Hang on tighter!**

The walls seem to be bulging. All of the color from Venus and the blue fog are filling the house. Trooper feels smaller, somehow, as my arms are holding him like a python with its next kill. I have to adjust my hold tighter. Trooper's arms are still around me. They have readjusted now, and his fingers are laced together with a better grip. Trooper has turned to look at me, almost eye to eye, through the colors and the fog. Whitey is shouting between big breaths, **It's ... happening. It's happen ... ing.** For a few more seconds, the whirling eddy speeds up to one final heart-stopping thrust. My eyes are squeezing shut, and my teeth are clenched. I remember this, and I know Trooper and Whitey are experiencing the same thing. We all are holding on so tight to each other, that it's painful. I can feel the little guy's bones and some muscle in his arms.

The clouds arrive. They are veiling Venus, and it's suddenly still and dark. I can hear us all breathing in different rhythms.

Nobody is saying anything for what seems forever. The Trooper isn't even whimpering, and he has let go of my middle. He's simply standing there between Whitey and me.

Whitey finally speaks in a normal voice. "Sit on the floor." As we're sitting there, we can hear thunder. I'm looking up at the half-wall, and I can tell that those clouds that were so far away a while ago, are now very near and moving closer very rapidly. We hear more thunder, and it's louder with lightening streaking downward like crooked daggers. In that flashing light, I'm getting quick glimpses of the Trooper. I can barely see the edge of the clouds. There are stars directly above, but our view of them is cut off as the clouds progress toward the east and the north. A blinding slash of lightening streaks downward, very near to us, followed by an ear-splitting crack of thunder that sounds like a million rocks sliding out of a giant drum and landing on a metal roof. There is a deafening boom, as a transformer blows.

"We gotta get out of here. Everybody up. I'll go first and guard the ground when you come down." Whitey moves the trap door cover and is down the ladder in seconds. I am in awe, as Trooper moves like a *cat*, hangs from the edge of the trap door, and drops to the ground, landing with knees bent. I'm seeing him spring back up to a standing position in a fraction of a second. Just like an athlete. Just like I did in 1949. He's waiting with Whitey while I make my way down the ladder. I spring off from the third step.

The three of us run for the side door, just as the power goes out, leaving my part of the city and my house in the dark. Big drops of rain are hitting the backs of our necks as we open the door. We're quickly up two steps and into the kitchen. Barnabus streaks between my legs, nearly causing me to fall. I'm leading them into the living room where we all find softer places to sit. There aren't any words to say yet. Whitey's hair is easy to see in the lightening flashes. He's sitting on the couch. The boy I know to be my grandson is sitting on the ottoman, running his fingers through his short hair with his head down and his elbows on his knees. I'm not in my recliner. I'm still standing, trying to recover and figure out what to say or do from this point.

"GO to him." Whitey whispers. I can hardly see, but the Trooper looks over at Whitey and then back to me. I'm not looking for flashlights or candles. I don't think I even *want* them right now. It would be too ... intrusive. That's the word. I take a couple of steps in the direction of my grandson, but I stop. I don't know what to say. I feel paralyzed.

"It's OK, Paw Paw. Come here." It's a soft, respectful voice. Trooper is comforting *ME*. I can't help myself, and I let out the most desperate choking sob. It doesn't even sound like me.

Whitey is silent, but his eyes are glowing.

I'm feeling braver now, so I move to Trooper, just as another blinding flash of lightening streaks down, followed by another louder crack of thunder that rattles the windows. I'm in front of him now, and I'm on my knees. "Trooper?" My hands are cradling his face. It's much thinner. I feel that he is smiling, but I can't tell for sure in the shadowy room. His head is like mine. Not smaller, as it was before. I feel further back and touch his ears that are now somehow higher. My hands are following the shape of his head down to his longer and thinner neck. I touch his mouth, which is shut. Not open as it would have been, usually. There is no wet, little tongue sticking out at me. He is looking me in the eyes, and I can tell that his eyes are wider and not slanted, when another flash of lightening shows them to me. I have my hands on his shoulders that are somehow broader now, and the sleeves of my T-shirt no longer hang down to his elbows.

His arms don't feel soft. There is a slight hint of defined muscle that I can detect in his teenage body. I'm taking his hands in mine. The fingers are much longer now. "Basketball, or piano?" I whisper, and I really don't know who I'm talking to at this moment, but at least I have found something to say.

"Baseball. Like you." I'm on the verge of another sob, but manage to control that.

"Stand up for me, will you, Trooper?" He stands and looks me directly in the nose. He's twelve. He's going to be quite a bit taller, I'm guessing. "Take your shoes off for me." Those Nikes that I gave him almost fit. He has narrow, long feet with no space between his big toe and the rest. "Those sweats are OK now, aren't they, Pal? They don't puff out at the bottom anymore."

"I need new stuff, I think." He says clearly, with words he would always use, but that vocabulary will grow fast, I know. He doesn't seem to know exactly what has happened. At this point, the ramifications of this life-changing night are becoming very apparent to me. I'm thinking of Wendy, and I'm at sea as to what I'm going to tell her. Do I call her now? Do I wait for tomorrow morning?

"You gotta call Wendy, Pal. No question." Whitey is right. I have no choice.

"Yes, let's call Mama." Trooper is trying to deal with a very different mind and body now. The sound of his own words seems to puzzle him.

"I'll call your Mama, Trooper. But first, do you mind if I light a candle? Is that OK, Trooper? I would like very much to see your face." *And not with a flashlight.*

"OK." Trooper is gazing at me and smiling.

I have found a couple of emergency candles in the kitchen along with some matches. Light helps. My heart is beating a hell of a lot faster than normal right now. Whitey has moved around so he can face Trooper, as I bring in my new source of light. I'm trying to be respectful in my eagerness to see that sweet face, but Trooper doesn't seem to mind my inspection. The flickering flame shows every hollow and angle of this handsome boy's slightly renewed, more mature face.

"He looks like you, my man."

I haven't thought about the fact that Trooper could resemble me. I could gaze at my grandson's face forever, but I know it's time to call Wendy.

She seems upset at the thought that I would need to call her.

"Is he sick, Daddy? TELL me!"

"No, he's not sick, Honey … He … has a surprise for you."

"What kind of susrprise?"

"You'll see, Sweetheart. By the way, we've had a power outage in the neighborhood from the storm. We're all fine. Whitey's here too."

"WHAT storm? I'm inside a bar, clear across town! There's loud music! How would I know there's a storm outside? Is Bernie Bern OK?"

"He's OK, but he really wants to talk to you. I think you should come."

"Dammit, Dad. Why can't you just TELL me so I can at least BRACE myself! I'm getting into the car right now. I'll be right there." I'm hoping that Whitey is right about people not being mad because of the *gift*, and I'm thinking I need another beer.

"I think I'll just mosey on home before Wendy gets here. This is a family thing. I'm feeling like an intruder." Whitey stands up.

"Oh no you don't, Pal! We've been through all of this together. You can't pull out on me now. I need you to be here."

"You got it, but I'm keeping quiet."

There's still thunder rumbling and lightening, but it seems to be moving east from here.

"Anybody want a potato chip and something to drink?"

"I want potato chips and a … pop." I'm witnessing a metamorphosis. Trooper didn't say "soda".

"How 'bout a beer?" Whitey isn't anxious to leave. I know that.

I wend my way back to the kitchen and quickly fish two beers and a can of Coke from my silent, dark refrigerator. The three of us are crunching and drinking comfortably. I'm lying. I'm not comfortable. I can't imagine my daughter's reaction. Maybe this beer will help me, if I get enough of it down before she arrives.

Trooper has moved from the ottoman to the opposite end of the sofa from where Whitey is seated. I'm in the recliner, but not for long. We hear a car door close, and I'm up, like that old jack-in-the-box, because I need to meet her at the door for some reason I can't explain.

"Hi, Dad. Where's Bernie Bern?" Wendy looks a little frantic.

"He's right in here, waiting for you." I'm trying to sound casual and relaxed, but inside it's a different story. "Be careful, Honey. It's dark here on the porch, but I have a candle lit in the front room."

Wendy starts to question me again, and I tell her to go on in. I can tell she's upset, not knowing what Trooper has to say to her.

"Hi, Sweetheart. Mama's h ...?" Wendy stops, just inside the door. She isn't able to speak, and she is taking in the vision of the twelve-year-old boy on the couch in the candlelight. I can tell that she is trying to process what she knows with what she sees. Her son is looking at her with expectant eyes. He seems self-conscious. Why wouldn't he be?

"Where's ... who is ..." She manages to make her feet carry her closer to the sofa. She's looking at a stranger who isn't a stranger, because there are things about the boy that she knows. And they are there, right before her eyes. She looks puzzled, and then not. Whitey and I are waiting quietly. I can see a faint smile on the Trooper's face in the candlelight. He glances over at me with happy anticipation in his eyes at the thought of his *new*, first words to his mother. Wendy is looking down at Trooper, but she's still not able to speak. It's all I can do to keep quiet. I have this great urge to end the silence, to break the tension, but it wouldn't be right. Whitey and I are only extras in this scene. We just watch.

When my grandson rises slowly from the sofa to stand facing his mother, Wendy takes a couple of steps back. There's something I hadn't realized until now. Trooper's eyes are level with his mother's. His prior, chunky little body was much shorter; I have to say, now that I see him next to his mom. Trooper's mouth is moving tentatively, as if he's figuring out what to say. I'm holding my breath. Wendy is softly sobbing, and I don't know if she knows why. I'm not sure she has a grip on what she is seeing.

"M ... m ... Mom. Don't cry, Mom. I'm cool. It's me. I'm OK."

My eyes are so full, that I'm having trouble seeing in the moving flame of the candle. Whitey's head is down, his elbows are on his knees and his hands are folded. He is setting himself somewhere else in his mind to offer privacy. Wendy releases a huge sob, as she throws her arms around the Trooper, who gives the giant hug right back to her. They're both laughing and crying at the same time. They're becoming quiet now, but still holding each other so tightly that they look like one person in the lightening flashes. It is a long silence before any more words are spoken. Sometimes words are an intrusion, but someone does speak, at last.

"Do you think maybe I could play baseball, Mom?"

EPILOGUE

Whitey is right. Happiness does come with the gift. Wendy is overwhelmed with it, and her time is filled with the joys of seeing Bernie (that's what he wishes to be called now) bloom with the help of many others who surround him. He's learning to bat and pitch and "dig 'em out of the dirt" coached by yours truly. He has inherited my old glove with my name in it.

I can feel the love of my daughter more than ever. Happy as she is, Wendy cherishes the photo albums of Trooper when he was a baby, more than ever now.

Whitey and I still have our breakfasts at Bucky's place, and Petty Cash still gives us the raspberries and threatens to blackmail us about the theft of the tree house from the Woodard property. Come to find out, she is a private investigator, in spite of my doubts.

I'm having a hard time getting my mind around what Whitey and I have done and what will happen in the future for all concerned, so I've dived into a small project that needs to be finished. It will be therapeutic for me, and it is my responsibility, after all. When I'm finished with the thing, it's gotta get back up in the tree house *zip spat* or I'll be dealing with the neighbors, the press and multi-colored beams shooting all over the place again.

SIMON WOODARD-JUNE 1924
WILMA WOODARD-JUNE 1926
KENNY WOODARD-JUNE 1944
DUANE SWIFT-JUNE 1946
WARREN HEARST-JUNE 1949
BERNARD (TROOPER) HEARST-APRIL 2008